THEY WERE STARING DOWN INTO A DEEP CHASM in the heart of the mountain.

In its center was a bustling village, lit by torchlight and wreathed in smoke.

"Beauty!" Nell suddenly cried. She pointed to a large, glowing white body making its way slowly down the mountainside.

"Hush!" Pim reminded her. "You're not back in Xandria, remember? You'd be wise to keep quiet, and out of sight."

Nell huffed in frustration. "But if I could just call her," she repeated. "What if we don't reach her in time? What if he plans to hurt her?"

"Think, Princess," Pim insisted. "If you call her, that bloke that's with her will instantly know we're here, and soon after, so will the whole village. Then what happens to your rescue plans? If you ever hope to be Imperial Wizard, you'd better get used to making hard choices."

Pim's words brought a little prickle of recognition.

"My Father told me that once," said Nell softly. "He didn't think I'd have the strength to make those choices."

"Was he right?" asked Pim.

Nell swallowed hard.

"No," she said. Then she started down the mountain-side, silently stealing from rock to rock, bush to bush. . . .

THE KEEPERS

The Dragonling Series

By Jackie French Koller

THE DRAGONLING COLLECTOR'S EDITION, Vol. 1

THE DRAGONLING COLLECTOR'S EDITION, Vol. 2

Available from Simon & Schuster

THE KEEPERS

BOOK TWO: The Wizard's Apprentice

By Jackie French Koller

ALADDIN PAPERBACKS
New York London Toronto Sydney Singapore

First Aladdin Paperbacks edition December 2003

ALADDIN PAPERBACKS
An imprint of Simon & Schuster
Children's Publishing Division
1230 Avenue of the Americas
New York, NY 10020

Designed by Debbie Sfetsios
The text of this book was set in Baskerville.

Printed in the United States of America
2 4 6 8 10 9 7 5 3 1

Library of Congress Control Number 2003107534

ISBN 0-689-85592-3

To Ginger—agent, fan, and friend

THE KEEPERS

BOOK TWO: The Wizard's Apprentice

FOREWORD

It is near the end of the First Chiliad[1] in the ancient
world of Eldearth. Graieconn, the Lord of Darkness is
still imprisoned in Darkearth, but he continues to build
up his forces, sending them above ground to wage war
on Eldearth and threaten the Scepter of Light, source of
all goodness. The Imperial Wizard, Keeper of the
Scepter, is old and weak. A new Keeper must be found,
but none of the candidates have succeeded in the quest,
until now. Princess Arenelle of Xandria has undertaken
the quest in secret, against her father's wishes, and she
has succeeded! But the old Wizard is loath to accept her
as his apprentice. Never in the history of Eldearth has
a girl become a Wizard, much less an Imperial Wizard.
Besides, she does not bear the Mark of the Dove as
foretold by the prophecy. Arenelle refuses to give in,
however, and the Imperial Wizard finally relents and
agrees to accept her, *if* she convinces her father, the

---

[1] Thousand Years

king, to bestow upon her the Mantle of Trust. The mantle is typically passed from father to son, or, when there is no son, to the nearest male relative. In this case, since Arenelle has no brother, it would be Lord Taman, Grand Court Wizard and nephew to the king. Nell returns home and ultimately persuades her father to relinquish the mantle, but just as he is about to bestow the mantle upon her, Lady Fidelia, Grand Court Witch and lady-in-waiting to the princess comes forth with a shocking revelation. . . .

CHAPTER ONE

Lady Fidelia and Lord Taman hurried into the library.

"You sent for us, sire?" said Lady Fidelia.

"Yes," said King Einar. His hand rested affectionately on Princess Arenelle's shoulder. "It seems that you were right about Arenelle, Lady Fidelia. She is special indeed. In fact she has completed the Wizard Quest!"

Lord Taman gasped.

Lady Fidelia's eyes widened. "Arenelle! I am amazed!" she said.

Nell smiled proudly.

"The Imperial Wizard has agreed to accept Arenelle as apprentice," the king went on, "providing that I bestow upon her the Mantle of Truth."

"The . . . the mantle," Lord Taman stammered. "But, sire . . ."

"I know it is unusual," said King Einar, "but obviously Arenelle is an unusual young woman. Lady Fidelia, please make the preparations for the Mantle Ceremony."

Lady Fidelia took a deep breath. "Before I do, sire," she said, "there is something you must know."

"What is that?" asked the king.

"There is another who may deserve to wear the mantle," said Lady Fidelia.

"Quite so," said Lord Taman.

"I do not refer to you, Lord Taman," said Lady Fidelia solemnly. "I refer to the king's son, Arenelle's twin brother."

Nell gasped, Lord Taman blanched, and the king's mouth fell open.

"What?" they blurted simultaneously.

"As you know," Lady Fidelia went on, "I was not only lady-in-waiting to Queen Alethia, but I was also her midwife."

"Yes," mumbled the king.

"Late in her pregnancy," said Lady Fidelia, "an old seer came to the queen. She told the queen that she carried twins, a boy and a girl, and that one of them, possibly even the girl, might fulfill the prophecy."

Nell's heart thumped.

"But," Lady Fidelia went on, "the seer also carried a warning. She told Queen Alethia that traitors at court were plotting, when and if she bore a boy child, to kidnap him and deliver him to Graieconn."

King Einar snapped to attention. "Traitors? What traitors?" he boomed. "Give me their names!"

"The seer could not divine their names or faces," said Lady Fidelia. "She could only feel the disruption in the balance between the darkness and the light, and sense their evil intent."

Lord Taman snorted. "This is utter nonsense," he contended.

"We will hear the whole of it," King Einar said, "before we decide what is and isn't nonsense." He nodded to Lady Fidelia. "Go on."

"Because I was to attend the birth, the queen took me into her confidence," said Lady Fidelia. "She bade me to keep the fact that she carried twins a secret. I was to announce to the court only the birth of the girl, then hide the boy child away."

"Hide him? Hide him where?" asked the King.

"In plain sight," said Lady Fidelia, "where the Dark Lord would never think to look for a prince: in the Lanes."

"The Lanes!" King Einar jumped to his feet. "Do you mean that *my* son, heir to the throne of Xandria and, in all likelihood, the future Imperial Wizard, has been raised in filth and squalor like a common street urchin?"

Nell stiffened, irritated both by her father's instant assumption that *if* there was a boy child, *he* must be the Chosen One, and by the offhanded reference to conditions in the Lanes.

"Perhaps we need to think about why *any* of our subjects live in filth and squalor, Father," she said.

King Einar gave her a quick, dismissive glance and returned to glaring at Lady Fidelia.

"And may I remind you," Nell pressed on, "that the

3

seer said that *I* might just as likely be the Chosen One."

"Come now, Cousin," said Lord Taman.

"Yes, Arenelle," King Einar chimed in. "It would seem that all is finally becoming clear. If in fact this is true, your brother must be the Chosen One. It must be he who bears the Mark of the Dove."

"I'm afraid not, sire," said Lady Fidelia. "The boy bears a Charm Mark, it's true, but it no more resembles a dove than Arenelle's does."

Nell smiled smugly.

Lord Taman's brow furrowed. "Where is this boy?" he said. "And why have you not brought him forth before this?"

Lady Fidelia flushed a bright shade of scarlet.

"I fear," she said haltingly, "that he is missing."

CHAPTER TWO

"Missing!" King Einar boomed.

Minna, Nell's small Demidragon, woke with a start. She darted from her perch near the fireplace into Nell's arms.

"Shhh," Nell comforted her. "It's all right."

King Einar threw his hands in the air. "What madness is this?" he raved. "First you tell me I have a son I've never known about, and then you tell me you've lost him?"

"Sire!" Lady Fidelia admonished. "Your voice! Do you wish the whole castle to hear?"

King Einar put his hands to his head and squeezed. "I don't know what I want," he said miserably. "My mind is spinning."

Nell's mind was spinning too. Did she really, truly have a brother? Her skin prickled with wonder. A real, flesh-and-blood brother of her own? How often over the years she had longed for a brother or sister to share her joys and sorrows with.

And yet if she did have a brother, then what of her chance to become Imperial Wizard? What of the mantle? Would her father automatically confer it upon this long lost son?

Minna hopped to the arm of Nell's chair, then fluttered to a nearby table and perched on the edge of a bowl of grapes. She gazed at Nell beseechingly.

Nell smiled and nodded, and Minna dove in.

Meanwhile Lord Taman had started to pace the room. "This tale grows wilder with each twist, Sire," he said. "Surely you don't believe it?"

King Einar shook his head. "I don't know what to believe," he said. "I'm still awaiting an explanation!"

Lady Fidelia sucked in a deep breath. "Yes, sire," she said. "Well, you see, the boy was raised in the home of an old woman in the Lanes, where I have been regularly visiting him in secret. The queen did not wish the boy's existence to be revealed until he was old enough to undertake his quest."

"That would have been several weeks ago," the king stated impatiently. "When he turned one-one."

"Yes," said Lady Fidelia, "and I went to see him on that day, but he was gone. The neighbors told me that the old woman had died and the boy had run off."

"How *inconvenient,*" Lord Taman quipped.

Nell's ears pricked up. So it *was* Lady Fidelia she had seen in the Lanes the night she had crept out and met the boy, Owen! And on the night that they had met, Owen had told Nell that *his* guardian had recently died.

She remembered having an eerie feeling that her meeting with Owen was somehow meant to be.

"I've been scouring the Lanes ever since," said Lady Fidelia, "but—"

"When you visited this boy," Nell interrupted. "Did you teach him to read?"

"Why, yes, of course," said Lady Fidelia. "I knew he would need to know how when the time came to reveal his true identity."

Nell stared, goose bumps prickling in the roots of her hair. "Did he call you Auntie?" she asked, "and did he call himself Owen?"

Lady Fidelia's jaw dropped. "Why, yes. How did you know?"

"I know him," said Nell. "I know him very well."

Lady Fidelia, King Einar, and Lord Taman all stared at her in disbelief.

"How?" they asked in unison.

"Remember how I told you I sent another to Madame Sofia's academy in my place?" Nell said to her father.

The king slowly nodded.

"That other is Owen."

The King's mouth fell open again.

"But how . . . ," he began

"It's a long story," said Nell.

"Are you sure of this?" asked Lady Fidelia wonderingly.

"Yes," said Nell. "In fact . . ." She reached under her

skirt, and pulled out the dagger Owen had given her.

Lady Fidelia gasped. "That is *his*!" she cried, coming over and taking the dagger into her hand. "Queen Alethia left it to him. How did you get it?"

"He loaned it to me, to protect me on my journey."

Lord Taman seemed speechless, for once. He stood silently, staring at the dagger, his brow creased in concentration.

The king was bewildered, too. He sat down and stared into nothingness, slowly shaking his head. The only sounds in the room were Minna's slurpy smacks as she munched on her grapes.

"I am worn out with trying to grasp all of this," King Einar muttered at last. "That Alethia would hide such a thing from me? My own son . . ."

"She did what she thought she had to do, sire," said Lady Fidelia.

The king sighed. "I suppose you are right," he said. "That is what I must believe. But now I would see my son! *My son*. What wondrous words." His eyes began to glow. "We are a family of three, Arenelle," he said. "Imagine . . ."

"Imagine . . . ," mumbled Lord Taman.

Nell could not help but feel a twinge of jealousy over the incredibly loving way that her father pronounced the word *son*. Now that he had a son, would a daughter mean less?

"Lord Taman," said the king suddenly. "We must send a party to retrieve my son at once!"

Lord Taman straightened. "Yes, sire," he said with a dip of his head, "but I fear the night is already upon us. I shall prepare a party to leave at dawn and I shall lead it myself."

"Sire," said Lady Fidelia. "If I may suggest . . ."

"Yes?" said the King.

"We do not know if the traitors that the seer warned of are still about. It would be best, perhaps, not to broadcast the boy's true identity quite yet."

The king nodded. "You are wise, Lady Fidelia." He turned to Lord Taman. "Simply let it be known that the boy is an imposter, posing as my daughter, and that he is being apprehended to face his discipline."

"As you wish, sire," said Lord Taman. He bowed and promptly left the room.

"I shall lend a hand with the preparations," said Lady Fidelia, hurrying after him.

"Father," said Nell, once they were alone. "What of the mantle? You will still grant it, will you not?"

King Einar crossed his arms over his chest and nodded slowly.

"Yes, I shall grant it," he said.

Nell smiled, relieved. "When?" she asked.

"When your brother arrives."

"But why? What has that to do with it?" Nell asked.

"It has *everything* to do with it," said King Einar, "since he is the one who shall be receiving it."

"What?" Nell cried. "You can't give Owen the mantle! He hasn't even undergone the quest."

"But he will," said King Einar. "And he will no doubt succeed."

"But *I* have already succeeded!" Nell declared.

King Einar threw up his hands.

"You were fortunate in your quest," he said. "Graieconn was unaware of your mission. That may no longer be the case. You are home safe now, and I intend to keep you that way. It was one thing when it seemed you were our only hope. But that has changed now. I have a *son*."

That incredulous look came into King Einar's eyes again as he voiced that word with reverence and awe.

"But—"

"No buts, Arenelle," King Einar commanded. "This conversation is at an end."

"Aargh!" Nell grunted. She spun on her heel and stomped out of the room.

Minna zipped over and hovered for a moment in front of the king.

"Pfft!" She spat a grape in his face, then turned and zoomed out the door after Nell.

"Why you impertinent little worm!" Nell heard her father bellow. "If I get my hands on you . . ."

CHAPTER THREE

Nell stormed through the castle corridors, her emotions in a muddle. One moment she was seething with anger and jealousy, the next she was awash with wonder.

"Can you believe Father?" she said, throwing a glance over her shoulder at Minna. "He doesn't even know Owen and he's willing to hand over the mantle, no questions asked. What if it's all a mistake? What if he's not even my brother? My *brother* . . ." She paused and shook her head. "Could that wild, impetuous boy really be my brother?"

"Graw?" said Minna.

"Princess!" Lady Fidelia suddenly appeared, stepping magically out of a tapestry.

Nell clutched at her chest.

"Lady Fidelia. You startled me."

"I'm sorry," Lady Fidelia whispered. She looked up and down the long hallway, then reached out and grabbed Nell's hand. "Come quickly. You're in grave danger."

11

"Danger?" Nell's heart began to thump. "What kind of danger?"

"I'll explain later. Just come!"

Lady Fidelia pulled Nell into the tapestry and Nell reached back and grabbed Minna, pulling her in too. They found themselves in a narrow, dark passageway.

"Rrronk," said Minna.

"What is this place?" Nell asked as she was hurriedly pulled along.

"A secret escape route," said Lady Fidelia. "The castle is riddled with them."

"Rrronk," Minna said again.

"It's all right, Minna," Nell consoled her. "We'll be out of here soon."

Minna refused to be comforted. She kept snorting nervously.

"I don't know why Minna is so anxious," said Nell worriedly. "Is Father all right? What's happening?"

"Your father is fine," said Lady Fidelia. "We've had word of a plot against your lives. He's already left the castle by another route. I'm bringing you to him."

"But . . . I just left him not five minutes ago," said Nell. "How can this have happened so fast?"

"It will all be explained later," said Lady Fidelia. "Now stop asking questions and hurry." She tugged harder on Nell's hand. They wound through dank passageway after dank passageway, up and down several slimy, twisting staircases.

"I can't believe I never knew of these tunnels," said Nell.

"No one knows of them," said Lady Fidelia, "except the king and the most trusted members of the court."

At last they came to a dead end, but Nell noticed a trapdoor in the ceiling.

"Hush now," whispered Lady Fidelia. She pushed the door up part way and peered out, then she pushed it the rest of the way. She climbed out and reached down to help Nell. Nell let Minna go, and, with a shriek of indignation, the little Dragon hurled herself at Lady Fidelia's head.

"Get off me, you wretched worm!" Lady Fidelia hissed, slapping the little Dragon hard.

Minna fell to the floor, then immediately righted herself and attacked again, belching a stream of flame at Lady Fidelia.

"Minna, stop!" Nell cried, climbing up out of the tunnel. "What has gotten into you?"

Lady Fidelia grabbed a hayfork and lunged at the Demi.

"No!" cried Nell. "Don't hurt her!" She grabbed Minna and held her tightly. "Minna. Calm down!" she cried as the little beast struggled in her arms.

Nell realized for the first time where she was: the tack room in the Dragon stables. She heard heavy footsteps and then the tack room door burst open. Galen, the Dragon Master, rushed in, then stopped in his tracks.

"Lady Fidelia? Princess?" he said. "What are *you* doing here?"

"We need a Dragon and fast!" said Lady Fidelia. "No questions!"

"But . . ."

"*No* questions!" Lady Fidelia repeated.

"Yes, my lady," said the Dragon Master. He backed out of the room with a confused look on his face.

"Come," said Lady Fidelia, grabbing Nell's wrist, "and keep that worm under control or I'll kill it!"

Nell's heart raced. This was all so strange. Lady Fidelia had never spoken to her in such a tone! Something felt terribly, terribly wrong.

Lady Fidelia tugged her out of the tack room. Galen was saddling Brahn, a large Ring-necked Dragon.

"Is . . . something wrong, my lady?" he asked.

"No," said Lady Fidelia shortly. "Just hurry!"

Just then the door at the front entrance of the stable opened and . . .

Nell gasped. "Lady Fidelia!" she cried.

Lady Fidelia, or a woman who looked exactly like her, froze in the doorway.

Galen looked from one Witch to the other.

"An imposter!" the woman who held Nell's hand cried out. "Stop her!"

"You're the imposter!" the other woman called out. "Nell! Stand aside!" She pulled out her wand.

It didn't take Nell long to decide which Witch was the imposter. No wonder Minna had been acting so strange!

Nell set Minna free and tried to break away from the imposter's grasp, but the woman only pulled her closer.

"Don't be a fool," the woman hissed. "*She* is the very danger I warned you about! Forgive me if I'm not acting myself, Princess, but I am wracked with fear for you and your father."

Nell hesitated. Now she was not so sure.

But Minna was.

With another scream the little Dragon flew at Nell's captor once again, sinking her claws into the arm that held Nell prisoner.

With a cry of rage the woman shook Minna loose, knocking her to the floor again. The little Dragon lay there gasping, the wind knocked from her small lungs. Then the imposter pulled out a wand of her own and pointed it at Minna.

"Lord of Darkness," she began to chant in a voice suddenly deep and guttural.

"No!" Nell cried. She grabbed hold of the wand and tried to twist it from the imposter's hand. A jolt of pain raced up her arm, and her hand opened and fell to her side, numb and useless.

The real Lady Fidelia was running toward her now, along with Galen the Dragon Master.

"Stand back!" the imposter declared, grabbing Nell around the neck. "Stand back or the princess dies."

Lady Fidelia and Galen stopped in their tracks.

Nell choked and gasped as the woman's grasp on her neck tightened.

"GRRRUMMM!" came another loud Dragon cry.

Out of the corner of her eye Nell could see her white Dragon, Beauty, thrashing angrily in her stall at the far end of the stable.

"Stay where you are," the imposter shouted to Lady Fidelia and Galen as she dragged Nell toward the saddled Ring-neck.

Nell struggled to reach the ruby pendant which encircled her neck, a protective amulet given to her by her mother, but her remaining good arm was pinned against her side.

"Rrronk!" came another cry, and then a blur of purple shot by Nell and hit the imposter fully in the face. The woman shrieked, and in that spilt second Nell broke free and ran to the arms of the real Lady Fidelia. Minna followed.

"Now *you* stay where you are!" Lady Fidelia directed the imposter. She leveled her wand at the woman.

The woman aimed her wand back.

Gently Lady Fidelia pushed Nell and Minna away.

"Lord of Darkness," the imposter began to chant.

"Lord of Light," Lady Fidelia countered.

Their incantations were interrupted by a brilliant light, and the imposter's wand burst into flames. She screamed and crumpled to the ground. Nell whirled to see Lord Taman standing in the doorway, his wand outstretched.

CHAPTER FOUR

Nell was still feeling trembly after her close call. The false Lady Fidelia had turned out to be a Wizard, her father's Minister of Magic, a trusted cabinet member who had been at the castle for many years. Was he the traitor her mother had been warned about? Were there others? It was all very unsettling.

"I think I'm going to go to bed early," she told her father at supper. "I feel very tired all of a sudden."

"Now do you see the dangers you are up against?" her father asked. "Do you understand why I wish to keep you under my wing?"

Nell was too tired to argue. "I just want to go to bed," she said quietly.

Her father nodded and kissed her head. "And you," he said, shaking a finger at Minna. Then he smiled and rubbed her head. "You can spit grapes at me any time you want, my little friend."

Minna chortled happily. She was quite enjoying being the hero of the hour.

Back in her room Nell stood before the portrait of her mother. The gentle face beamed loving warmth upon her. It looked so real, almost alive. Nell reached inside her bodice and took hold of the enchanted pendant.

"I'm frightened, Mother," she said. "I'm frightened and tired and discouraged. Should I even continue to try? What would you have done?" The pendant grew warm in her hand and pulsed, giving her strength and courage. She knew, of course, what her mother would have done. Her mother would have done whatever Eldearth required of her. . . .

And that's what Nell would do. She dressed in her nightgown and pulled back her bed curtains. Minna fluttered in and curled up on her pillow. Nell smiled, her heart swelling with tenderness toward the little Dragon.

"Would that I had your courage, little friend," she whispered.

Minna yawned, her forked tongue uncurling, then curling up again. She snuggled down and closed her eyes.

Nell sighed. "I suppose I had better contact Owen before I go to bed and tell him Lord Taman is coming for him," she said.

But Minna was already asleep.

Nell had given away her new speaking star, but she knew she had an old one somewhere. She rummaged through her desk drawers until she found it. The speaking star was a bit tarnished and scratched, but she was sure it would still work. She rubbed it until it shone dully, then she stared into it.

"Owen," she said, "at Madame Sofia's."

The star started to slowly glow. Colors swirled, then gradually took shape. Owen's room appeared. Owen stood in its center with a group of girls huddled around him. What on Eldearth was he doing now? As long as Nell didn't speak, the star allowed her to observe him unnoticed. Nell zoomed in on him, noticing once again how much his features were like hers.

"My brother," she whispered, warming to the words in spite of herself. Owen had some sort of a uniform on, a long plaid pinafore with a puffy-sleeved white blouse. His shoulder-length hair was pulled back and fastened with a ribbon. Nell giggled.

Owen's head suddenly cocked to the left, and he stopped speaking midsentence. Nell knew he had heard her laugh.

"Owen," she whispered quickly. "I need to talk to you. Can you find some privacy?"

Owen blinked slowly to show he had heard.

"Umm, excuse me," he said in his feigned female voice to the sea of faces below him. "I have to pee."

Then he darted through his dressing room, into his water closet. Behind him a chorus of tittering broke out.

"Are you crazy?" Nell said to him. "You can't say things like that."

"Like what?" asked Owen.

"Like . . . pee," said Nell.

"Of course I can," said Owen. "I say it all the time. Sometimes I say worse."

Nell blushed. "I mean you can't say it when you're pretending to be me," she reprimanded. "I would never say anything like that."

"What do you say then, when you have to?" asked Owen.

"I say I have a little business to take care of," said Nell.

Owen humphed. "Remind me never to do business with you," he said.

Nell grimaced. "Very funny," she said. "What were you doing back there anyway?"

"Planning a rebellion," said Owen.

"A rebellion?" said Nell. "Against what?"

"Against these silly frocks they make us wear to play glowball," said Owen. "It's ridiculous. Our legs get all tangled up in the skirts—especially mine."

"Well, what else would you wear?" asked Nell.

"Trousers, of course," said Owen.

"Trousers!" Nell laughed out loud. "You don't actually think they'll ever allow the novitiates at the Academy of Witchcraft to wear trousers!"

"I do," said Owen. "And that's just the beginning. I'm going to change a lot of things around here."

"Oh, no, you're not," said Nell.

"Yes, I am. You just watch me," said Owen.

"Well, I'll admit that might be something to see," said Nell, "but you're not going to be around there much longer. Lord Taman and some of the guards are coming to pick you up in the morning."

"Why?" asked Owen. "Are you all done with whatever you had to do?"

"No," said Nell, "but it's not a secret anymore."

"Are you in trouble?" asked Owen.

"No," said Nell, "but you are."

"What?" said Owen. "Why?"

"Well, you're not really," said Nell. "But the guards think you are, so just play along and we'll explain everything to you when you get back here."

"Are they going to put me in a dungeon or anything?"

Nell giggled. "Not if you cooperate."

"Okay," said Owen. "Just remember, you promised to help me get into Wizard University when I get back."

"Yes," said Nell. "Well, you'll have to take that up with Father. He has . . . other plans for you."

"What do you mean other plans?" asked Owen suspiciously. "Does me being a Wizard figure into these plans?"

Nell chuckled wryly.

"Does it *ever*," she said.

Chapter Five

Nell was awakened by a commotion outside her window. She sat up and rubbed her eyes, still exhausted. Lying open on the bed beside her was *The Wizard's Pocket Companion*. She had snuck into Lord Taman's library and borrowed it last night, fighting to keep her eyes open, studying spells. She had worked on a sleeping spell until she'd finally succumbed to sleep herself.

As Nell climbed out of bed, a little Gremlin scurried across the floor. She pointed at it and concentrated hard.

"Fall asleep, soft and deep," she said. "Close your eyes against the sun. Do not wake till day is done."

The little Gremlin's steps slowed. It's tail started to drag, then it curled up into a little ball and started snoring.

Nell smiled, immensely pleased with herself.

From outside came the sounds of voices, of Dragons blowing and snorting. Nell went to the window, unbolted the shutters, and looked out. In the yard below, Lord Taman and the Dragonguard were preparing to take off.

Ah, yes, Nell remembered. *The precious* son. She prickled a bit with irritation. Lord Taman would retrieve the boy and be back by nightfall. And then the mantle would be bestowed upon Owen, the mantle that rightfully belonged to her.

There was a knock on her chamber door, and Nell turned.

"Who is it?" she called impatiently.

"Your maidservant, my lady, come to help you dress for breakfast."

"I don't want any help," Nell snapped. "Tell Cook I'll have breakfast to my room."

"As you wish, my lady."

A short time later there was another knock at the door.

"Who is it now?" Nell asked.

A small jingle was the only reply. Nell opened the door to find a covered tray floating there. She lifted the lid. Roasted eggs, a bingleberry muffin, and a big bowl of mush with honey.

"On my desk, please," Nell said, and the tray floated across the room and settled down as directed.

Nell was about to close the door again when she saw a steaming mug of Unicorn milk floating down the corridor. She held out her hand, and the mug glided into it.

"Mmmmm," Minna stretched and fluttered her

wings. The tantalizing aroma of food had awoken her. She left her nest of quilts, whizzed over, and hovered hopefully above the bingleberry muffin.

Nell smiled. "Go ahead. Help yourself. I'm not hungry."

"Thrummm," sang Minna, diving into the tray. Soon crumbs were flying in all directions. Nell sipped her hot milk and walked again to the window. Lord Taman and the Dragonguard had already taken off. They were just a dark mass in the distance now, winging their way westward to Madame Sofia's.

Nell thought again of all the adventures she had faced on her quest, all the Folk she had met and all the promises she had made. Somehow she *had* to fulfill them. She remembered the way Talitha, the Trog slave, had laughed at her and called her a daft little thing for thinking she could make a difference. Was Talitha right? Was she just a daft little thing with a foolish dream?

"No!" she said out loud, banging her mug down on the windowsill and sloshing milk all over.

"Graw?" cried Minna.

Nell looked over at her. Minna was perched on the edge of the bowl of mush, her chin dripping honey. She blinked at Nell guiltily.

Nell chuckled. "I wasn't saying no to you, silly," she said. "Go ahead. You're a hero, remember? Eat all you want."

"Thrummm," sang Minna, her head plunging below the rim of the bowl again.

Another knock came on the door.

"Now what?" Nell said impatiently. "I didn't order anything else." She stomped across the room and pulled the door open. Lady Fidelia was standing there.

"Oh, it's you," Nell said flatly.

"May I come in?" Lady Fidelia asked.

"Why not?" Nell pulled the door open wider.

"You seem a bit out of sorts this morning," said Lady Fidelia.

"It's Father," said Nell. She walked over and threw herself across her rumpled bed. "Why is he so stubborn and so old-fashioned, Lady Fidelia?"

Lady Fidelia closed the door behind her and walked over to the bed. She picked up *The Wizard's Pocket Companion* and gave Nell a knowing smile.

"You'll be a Wizard one way or the other, eh?" she said.

Nell shrugged.

"Try not to be angry with your father, Princess," said Lady Fidelia.

"But he promised me the mantle, then he went back on his word," said Nell.

"Well, circumstances changed," said Lady Fidelia. "You can't blame him for that."

"And you," said Nell. "I thought you wanted me to succeed."

"I want you to have the same chance as your brother," said Lady Fidelia. "That is what your mother would have wanted."

Nell sat up cross-legged, hugging her pillow. "But I *don't* have the same chance," she said earnestly, "now that you stopped the Mantle Ceremony."

"I could not let your father make that choice without knowing the truth," she said. "That would have been unfair."

"And is it fair that he should choose Owen solely because he's a boy?" asked Nell.

Lady Fidelia sighed. "No," she said, "it is not, but he does seem steadfast in his decision."

Nell crossed her arms over her chest and huffed.

"Perhaps you should return to the Wizard and ask him to accept you without the mantle," Lady Fidelia suggested.

Nell shook her head. "He's as stubborn as Father," she said. "And even if I did wish to try again, I'm not even sure I remember how to get there."

"But your white Dragon remembers," said Lady Fidelia. "Once a Dragon has flown somewhere, the way is imprinted upon its mind. It can always return to any place it's been to once."

"But Beauty wasn't with me on the first part of the journey," said Nell, "and the Wizard sent us back here by magic."

"You still flew and you still covered the same territory," said Lady Fidelia. "The magic just speeded you through time."

"Really?" said Nell. "Can you make that kind of magic, Lady Fidelia?"

"Oh no!" Lady Fidelia laughed. "Time-transport takes a very strong spell. But I'll bet the Palace of Light is not so long a journey as the Dragon flies, even without magic."

"Do you really think so?" said Nell.

"I do," said Lady Fidelia. "I'll bet you could make it in a day."

"But how?" asked Nell. "Father is never going to let me fly out of here on a Dragon, and they don't make vanishshrouds *that* big."

"If I know you," said Lady Fidelia with a wink, "you'll find a way."

Another knock came on the door.

"*Now* who?" asked Nell petulantly.

"Arenelle," boomed King Einar's voice. "What's this nonsense about you not coming down to breakfast?"

Chapter Six

Nell put on her riding habit and tucked Owen's dagger under her belt.

"C'mon, Minna," she said. "We have to go appease Father and have some more breakfast."

"Thrummm," said Minna, zooming over to the door.

Nell laughed. "I wouldn't think you could fit another morsel in," she said, playfully poking Minna's round belly.

Minna chortled happily, then fluttered after Nell down to the breakfast room.

King Einar was already seated. He frowned when he saw Nell.

"I hope you don't think you're going riding, Arenelle," he said. "I have no intention of letting you out of my sight again any time soon."

Nell sighed. "Father, please," she said. "I just want to exercise the yearling. The Dragon Master said regular exercise would be an important part of her therapy."

"There are plenty of pages," said the king. "Let one of them exercise her."

Nell bristled. "Beauty has been through a great deal," she said. "She needs to be handled gently, by someone she trusts. If Ebb had been through as much, I'm sure you wouldn't trust his care to a page."

Ebb was King Einar's Dragon, a handsome Great Blue, of whom the king was inordinately fond.

King Einar pulled at his chin thoughtfully.

"All right then," he said. "But Galen is to accompany you. I do not want you flying alone."

"Even if I stay within sight of the palace?" Nell wheedled.

"Even so," the king declared firmly.

"Beauty!" called Nell, running down between the stalls of the Dragon stable.

The young Dragon swung its head around.

"Oh, look at you!" cried Nell. She climbed up and leaned over the gate of Beauty's stall. "You look wonderful!"

Minna zoomed past Nell into the stall.

"Thrummm," Minna sang. She hovered in front of the big Dragon's face and rubbed her tiny nose against Beauty's big one.

"Grrrummm," Beauty returned.

And she was a beauty! Her white scales gleamed, reflecting the pale light that streamed in through the high stable windows. Each scale was like a miniature rainbow, catching and breaking the light into a whole spectrum of colors. Her great lavender eyes were clear and shining, and she stood tall and straight, giving no hint that she had been near death just a few days earlier.

"What do you think of your worm now, eh?"

Nell turned and saw Galen walking toward her with a proud grin on his face.

"You are a magician!" cried Nell.

"That I am," said Galen, "but your girl there had a powerful will to get well, too. Thought all the excitement last night might set her back, but it didn't. Don't know when I've seen such a fighter."

Nell smiled and rubbed Beauty's thick neck.

"She's had to be a fighter to survive as long as she has," Nell told Galen.

"Ay," said Galen. "That's the truth. An albino's usually killed at birth. Its own mother'll do it in."

"Why?" cried Nell, aghast.

"It's kinder," said Galen, "than letting the others torture it slowly."

Nell looked at Beauty with sorrow. "That's what was happening to her when I found her," she said. "Why are the others so cruel, Galen?"

"It's nature's way to be suspicious of anything different," said Galen. "Animals have no compassion for the sick or the weak."

"I don't believe that," said Nell. She reached up and stroked Beauty's muzzle. "I'll bet your mother had compassion, didn't she, Beauty? I'll bet she sheltered you as long as she could. That's how you grew to be a yearling. That's why you came to me. You recognized love when you saw it. You'd known it before."

Beauty blinked her gentle eyes. Dragons had great powers of perception. Though they were nonverbal, they quickly picked up on feelings and emotions, and the brighter ones even understood mind pictures. Nell knew Beauty understood what she was saying.

"You had a strong mother, didn't you, girl?" Nell went on. "Like me." She caressed her mother's ruby pendant, feeling its warmth and power surge through her.

"You could be right," said Galen. "This critter gets her courage from somewhere. A mother's love's as good an answer as any I can fathom."

Nell smiled. "Can I exercise her?" she asked.

"Ay, but I'll have to go with you," said Galen. "Your father sent orders that you're not to go anywhere without an escort."

Nell huffed. "I know, but I don't see why he doesn't trust me."

Galen smiled wryly. "My guess is you *do* know why, Princess."

Nell crossed her arms in front of her chest. "Oh, all right then," she said. "When can we go?"

"In a bit. I've a few chores to finish up, then I'll saddle my worm and meet you in the paddock."

"Okay," said Nell. "I'll be waiting."

She put a sidesaddle and neck harness on Beauty, then took the reins and led the yearling outdoors.

Minna took up her favorite perch atop Beauty's head, looking like a little purple cock's comb.

Nell glanced up at the pale blue sky. She was tempted to mount Beauty and just take off for the Palace of Light, but she knew the alarm would sound and the guards would be after her in a thrice. If she could just slip away from Galen somehow, once they were out of sight of the castle.

You'll think of something, Lady Fidelia had said. "But what?" Nell asked out loud. She sat down on a rock and pondered.

Beauty grazed contentedly on the tufts of grass that poked through the paddock's fence. Minna played hide-and-seek with a little quail in the bushes on the other side.

"Awk!" Beauty suddenly cried. She reared back, and Nell jumped up. Something red poked up momentarily out of the tufts of grass that Beauty had been munching, but when Nell went over for a closer look, she saw nothing.

Beauty lowered her head again and took another tentative bite of grass.

"Yi!" came a small cry. A little red blur sped along the fence and disappeared into another clump of grass.

"What on Eldearth was that?" Nell wondered aloud. Then she remembered something she had learned on her quest, something Saidi, her little Nebbish friend, had said.

"Weefolk live everywhere," Saidi had told her. "Tallfolk just don't see them."

Nell ran over and dropped to her knees in the grass.

"Hello, there. Are you all right?" she asked.

No answer.

"Beauty didn't hurt you did she?"

Still no answer.

"Because she didn't mean to, I'm sure. She just didn't see you."

"Ar," a small voice grumbled. "Nobody ever sees the likes of us."

"*I* saw you," said Nell. "At least I caught a glimpse. I'd like to make your acquaintance, though."

"Why?" the voice asked skeptically.

"I'm hoping you might be able to help me," said Nell.

A small face peeked up out of the grass. It was an Imp, a jolly-looking little man, just a few inches tall, with a bushy white beard and round red cheeks. He wore a red cap, a plaid vest and brown leather britches.

"Me help you?" said the Imp with an irritated frown. "Why should I? Your worm there just about bit my head off."

"Well, you should have made some noise or something," said Nell. "What were you doing in that grass, anyway?"

"Oh!" said the man, putting his hands on his hips. "Like I don't have a right to be in a clump of grass? I suppose all the clumps of grass on Eldearth belong to the Tallfolk!"

"I didn't mean it like that," said Nell.

"How did you mean it, then?" asked the man, jutting out his chin.

"I meant that I would think a clump of grass in a Dragon paddock would not be a wise place for someone of your . . . size to be hanging about."

"Did it ever occur to you that this Dragon paddock *might* have been an Imp village before you Tallfolk fenced it in and stole it?"

"Well, no, I'm afraid it didn't."

"Well, it was. And for your information what I was doing in that clump was visiting the grave of my sainted mother, who was stepped on by one of your worms."

"Oh!" said Nell. "How awful! I'm so terribly sorry."

"Ar. Well, sorry won't bring 'er back, will it?"

Nell sucked in a deep breath and let it out slowly. "I had no idea," she said. "How long has this type of . . . thing been going on?"

"Centuries," said the man.

"Why don't you all raise a ruckus about it?" asked Nell.

"We have," said the man. "We've raised plenty of ruckuses, but it does no good. Tallfolk don't see us, don't hear us. We're invisible to the likes of you, except to some of the children—the ones with imagination. They see us, but grown-ups never believe them, so by the time they grow up, they become blind to us, too." Then he smiled. "We have ways of getting you back, though."

"Like what?" asked Nell.

"Like stealing stockings from the laundry—just one of a pair—moving spectacles, tying knots in the mending thread, draining the milk jug and putting it back in the icehouse empty, pushing the paddock gate open and letting the livestock out—lots of little things that drive Tallfolk crazy."

"Ah." Nell laughed. "That explains a lot."

There was a flutter of wings, and Minna landed close beside Nell. The little Dragon and the Imp looked at each other, both a bit startled.

"A Demi!" whispered the Imp. "Don't move! You'll frighten her away!"

Nell laughed. "No, I won't," she said. "She's quite tame." To prove her point Nell reached out and scratched Minna's head.

"Thrummm," Minna hummed.

"Well, I'll be bugsnuggled!" said the Imp. "How'd you tame her like that?"

"I didn't tame her," said Nell, "any more than she tamed me. We just became friends."

The Imp eyed Nell thoughtfully.

"Hmm," he said. "Could be there's more to you than meets the eye. And there's quite a bit that meets the eye—at least to the likes of me."

Nell smiled.

"Do you think she'd let me touch her?" asked the Imp. "I've always admired Demis."

"Don't know," said Nell. "You can try."

The Imp stepped forward tentatively.

"Hey there," he said, putting his hand out, palm up to Minna.

Minna stared at the small hand warily, but did not shy away.

"What's her name?" asked the Imp.

"I call her Minna," said Nell.

"Minna," said the Imp. "You're a little beauty, aren't you, Minna?" He reached up and touched Minna's cheek softly, then he slid his hand down and scratched her under the chin.

Nell watched carefully, remembering how Owen had tried to grab Minna the first time he'd gotten close enough. This little man seemed truly gentle.

"Do you think maybe she might let me ride her?" the Imp asked. "I've ridden lots of birds and butterflies, but I've always dreamed of riding a Dragon."

"You've never ridden a Dragon?" Nell asked.

"Well, I've stowed away on a few big ones, but it's not like riding one of your own, one just your size."

"She might let you," said Nell, "if I asked her to."

The Imp's eyes lit up. "Will you then?" he asked.

"Depends," said Nell.

"On what?"

"On whether you're willing to help me or not."

The Imp pulled at his beard and looked at her through narrowed eyes.

"Help you how?" he asked.

"There is someplace I need to go," said Nell "but my

father won't let me out of sight. Galen, the Dragon Master, is coming out shortly to ride with me. Once we get away from the castle and out of town, I need to slip away from him."

"Why?" asked the Imp.

"It's a long story," said Nell. "But I promise you this: If you help me, I will do everything in my power to make Eldearth safer for Weefolk."

The Imp looked unimpressed.

"Well, you don't look that powerful to me, and I don't know any reason why I should believe anything you say. But I *do* want that Dragon ride." He put out his hand. "Name's Archibald Pim," he said, "but folks just call me Pim. It's a better fit." He grinned.

Nell smiled too. She took the hand carefully between her thumb and forefinger and gently shook it.

"Lady Arenelle, Princess of Xandria," she said, "but folks call me Nell. Same reason."

CHAPTER SEVEN

"Here's the plan," said Pim. "I'll ride with the Dragon Master and when you give the word, I'll force him to land."

"How will you do that?" asked Nell.

"Leave it to me," said Pim with a cocky grin. "I've got my ways."

"You're not going to hurt him, are you?" asked Nell. "He's a good man."

"Nah. Just irritate him a bit." He reached down, filled both his hands with dirt, and stuffed them in his pockets.

"What's that for?" asked Nell.

"You'll see," said Pim. "Just send the Demi to pick me up once I force him down." He looked at Minna. "Have you got a saddle for her?"

"I'm afraid not," said Nell, "nor a neck halter, but you can use this." She untied her hair ribbon. "We'd better practice. Minna's never done this before. At least, not since I've known her.

"Look, Minna," she said, "I'm going to make you a halter, like Beauty's." She stood up and went over to tug on Beauty's halter. She then made a couple of knots in the ribbon and slipped it over Minna's head and down her neck, tightening it just enough so it was snug, but wouldn't restrict Minna's breathing.

"Graw?" said Minna, tilting her head first one way, then the other. She looked up at Beauty.

"That's right," said Nell. "You look just like a big Dragon now. And you know how I ride Beauty?" Nell touched Beauty's saddle and made a picture in her mind of herself riding, then she stared into Minna's eyes until she saw the light of understanding. "This is Pim," Nell went on, gesturing to Pim to come over. She handed him the two ends of the hair ribbon. "Pim would like a ride like that." Nell rubbed Minna's shoulder bones. "Would it be okay if he sat here?"

Minna looked at Pim skeptically.

"Pim is our friend," said Nell. "He wants to help us."

"That's right," said Pim, reaching out and gently stroking Minna's neck. "I'm right fond of Dragons."

"Watch, Minna," said Nell. She looked up at Beauty. "Mount, Beauty," she said.

Beauty lowered her head until her shoulders were almost touching the ground. Nell climbed into the saddle.

"Now you," she said to both Minna and Pim.

"Mount, Minna," said Pim.

Dutifully Minna lowered her head, and Pim climbed

up and seated himself between her shoulder blades. "Good girl," he said, patting her neck.

"Good girl," Nell repeated.

Minna raised her head. "Thrummm," she hummed.

"Uh-oh. Here comes Galen," Nell said suddenly. "You'd better hide, Pim."

"No need," said Pim, sliding spryly down Minna's back to the ground. "He won't see me."

"Are you sure?" said Nell.

"Bet my life on it," said Pim.

"Ready, Princess?" called Galen. He walked up to Nell, leading his Great Blue Dragon.

"Um . . . yes," said Nell.

Bold as day, Pim walked right between Galen's legs. He grabbed hold of the Dragon's reins and climbed hand over hand up to the Great Blue's halter.

Galen never blinked.

"Amazing," said Nell.

"What's amazing?" asked Galen.

"Um . . . I'm still amazed at what a great job you did healing Beauty," said Nell. "She's the picture of health!"

"Ay," said Galen. "Well, let's give her a good workout and keep her that way, shall we?"

"Come, Minna," Nell called. Minna took to her customary perch on Beauty's head.

Galen climbed into his saddle, taking no notice of Pim leaning jauntily against the Great Blue's crown horn.

"Away!" Galen called, and the Great Blue crouched and sprang.

"Away! Nell echoed, and Beauty did the same, her lovely white wings unfurling and sweeping great billows of air beneath them as she rose. Clouds of dust swirled across the paddock in their wake.

Beauty picked up speed and Nell's heart raced. The wind whipped through her hair as the village rushed by below. She'd never ridden a Dragon so smooth, so sleek! She almost felt as if she were a part of Beauty, as though she had wings of her own. Soon they were in the outlying farmlands where Unicorn herds grazed and fields of barley rippled in the breeze like swells on a golden sea.

"How does she sit?" called Galen.

"Like a dream!" cried Nell. "Race?"

"Race?" Galen laughed. "She's half my worm's size. We'll outdistance you in three wingbeats!"

"Have at it then!" cried Nell. She lifted the reins to give Beauty her head. "Fly, Beauty! Fly!"

Beauty surged ahead and wind filled Nell's mouth and snatched her breath away. She hunkered down to keep from being blown off. The village retreated farther into the distance, and the farmlands sped by in a blur of green and gold.

Galen's Great Blue was right alongside, its giant wings rising and falling in rhythmic beats. It shot ahead hundreds of yards with each stroke. But it was not passing them. Beauty was holding her own!

"Faster, Beauty! Faster!" Nell cried, flattening herself against the Dragon's neck.

Beauty stretched out like an arrow and sliced through the air. Slowly she started nosing ahead of the Great Blue. Then they were pulling away!

"All right, all right! Pull up!" Galen called. "You've made your point."

With a triumphant laugh Nell reined Beauty in. The graceful Dragon brought her head up and slowed.

"That's my Beauty," said Nell, patting the Dragon's thick neck.

Galen came alongside.

"She's not even winded!" Nell cried.

"She's *something*, I'll admit," said Galen, obviously impressed. "Never seen the likes!"

Nell caught a glimpse of Pim peering at her from behind the Great Blue's horn. She looked back. They were far out of town now, and the castle was nowhere in sight. She took a deep breath and reached up to pet Minna—their sign.

A few moments later she heard Galen cry out.

"Aach!" he shouted rubbing his eyes with the back of his arm. "Must of flown through a dust cloud. I can't see a thing. You all right, Princess?"

"Yes, I'm fine," said Nell. "Maybe it was a swarm of bugs."

"Whatever it was, we'd better put down for a while. I can't open my eyes."

The Great Blue was already spiraling downward.

Nell followed.

The Blue touched down, but Nell stayed aloft, slowly

circling until she saw Pim swing down and run clear.

"Minna," she said, pointing. "Go to Pim."

Minna zoomed down and Pim sprang to her back, grabbing the reins.

"Away!" he cried.

Minna shot into the air like a little pro. Soon she was flying proudly alongside her great, white friend.

"The Palace of Light, Beauty," said Nell. She formed a picture of the palace in her mind and concentrated hard. Then she let the reins go slack and gave Beauty her head. The Dragon banked, turned, and headed purposefully toward the far western mountains.

"Princess?" Nell heard Galen calling from below. "Princess? Where are you?"

CHAPTER EIGHT

"Wahoo!" shouted Pim. "This is some fun!"

Nell laughed.

"Glad you're enjoying yourself," she said, "but I think you two had better hitch a ride for a while. I've been flying slowly for Minna's sake, but I need to pick up the pace a little."

"As you wish," said Pim.

He guided Minna in for a landing on Beauty's head, then he hopped off.

"You're quite spry for . . . um . . . for . . ."

"An old man," said Pim with a merry chuckle.

"Well, I didn't mean . . . that is . . ."

"Yes, you did mean *old*," said Pim, "but don't worry. No offense taken. I'm only a hundred and two. I guess that seems old to you, but we Imps can live a couple hundred years or more. So I'm still a young pup." He gave Nell a wink.

Nell smiled. "Thanks for your help back there," she said. "That dust was a great idea."

"Often it's the simple ideas that work the best," said Pim. "Where are we going, anyway?"

Nell hadn't thought ahead as to what she was going to do with Pim once she escaped from Galen. She couldn't risk taking him back to the village, so it looked as if she were going to have to take him with her.

"We're going to the Palace of Light," she said.

"Oh righto," Pim mocked. "And what are we going to do there? Have tea with the Imperial Wizard?"

"Something like that," said Nell.

Pim looked at her dubiously.

"You're not serious, are you?" he said.

"I am," said Nell.

"Nobody knows how to get to the Palace of Light," said Pim.

"Nobody but me," said Nell smugly.

"Right," said Pim sarcastically. "Now, where are we *really* going?"

"Wait and see," said Nell.

She was a bit amazed herself as the day wore on and Beauty winged her way over many of the places Nell had visited on her quest.

"There's the Oldenwood," she called out, "and the waterfall! This must be the mountain I came through."

She shuddered at the memory of the night she had spent in a vermin-infested cave beneath that mountain.

Now they were over the blue valley of Cerulea. Nell worried about Talitha and Leah, the two women she had befriended there. She had given them her vanishshroud to help them escape from Leah's cruel husband, Orson. Nell longed to know if they had been successful, but she couldn't risk visiting the valley and being caught by the Trogs again.

"Hey, Princess," said Pim, patting his belly. "If I'da known we were going to be flying all day I'd have packed a lunch. Don't Dragons and princesses get hungry?"

Nell laughed.

"Now that you mention it, yes. My stomach is feeling pretty hollow, and I'm sure the Dragons could use some water and food, too. There's a lake not far ahead. We'll stop there."

Beauty cleared the mountains on the far side of Cerulea and soared out over the plains of Azwan. Nell kept an eye out for Arduans, roving bands of outcasts infected with the dread disease, Bloodpox. She was anxious to see Raechel, the little Arduan girl she had met on her first trip through Azwan, but there was no sign of any tent city.

"There's the lake!" she called at last. "Down, Beauty."

Beauty swept in a graceful arc to the lake's shore. Nell swung down out of the saddle, then helped Pim to the ground.

"Awful lot of big animal tracks around here," he said, standing on the edge of a great cat track and looking down into it. "You sure it's safe?"

"Yes," said Nell. "Those are just the Hinterbeasts—"

"*Just* the Hinterbeasts!" cried Pim. "Is your mind addled? A pack of Hinterbeasts would make short work of Beauty, let alone me!"

"Not if you know how to charm them," said Nell, "and I do."

Pim shook his head doubtfully. "You got *some* imagination there, Princess," he said.

Nell just smiled. "Come on," she said. "Let's have a drink."

Minna and Beauty were already greedily gulping at the water's edge. Nell knelt and scooped up several great handfuls and Pim did the same.

"It sure is nice to be able to eat and drink at will again," said Nell. "On the quest I was allowed but one parse of water per day, and no food."

"What quest is that?" asked Pim.

"Never mind," said Nell. "You wouldn't believe me anyway."

Minna and Beauty had wandered off toward a thicket in the distance.

"Let's follow Minna," said Nell. "She found some delicious-looking nuts and berries when we were here last."

"Mind if I hitch a ride?" asked Pim. "That thicket may not look far off to you, but to me it looks like a half day's hike."

Nell laughed.

"Sure," she said, "but this is new to me. Where do you usually . . . ride a person?"

"It's new to me too," said Pim, "but that waterskin of yours looks like it might do."

"All right then," said Nell. She put her hand down and Pim hopped onto it, then she lifted him to her waist. He climbed onto her waterskin and straddled it like a saddle.

"Nice view up here," he said. "You're even prettier up close than you are from a distance. What do you say, Princess—you and me? We'd make a handsome couple, don't you think?"

Nell giggled.

"What?" said Pim in a wounded voice. "You think I'm kidding? Why, if I were fifty years younger, I'd ask for your hand."

Nell laughed. "And what about the rest of me?" she said.

"Well, I'd ask for that, too," said Pim with a little swagger in his voice. "Only . . . I'm not sure what I'd do with it all."

They both laughed.

"Grape?" said Nell.

They had reached the thicket and followed Beauty and Minna to a tangle of vines, heavy with grapes.

"Don't mind if I do," said Pim, grasping the fruit with both hands. "Oof! Heavy one. Better sit down."

Suddenly a dark shadow fell across the thicket.

Nell looked up.

"A Skreek!" shouted Pim, diving off the waterskin into the brush. "Hide!"

But there was no time. Before Nell could scramble for cover, the giant buzzard was upon them. With it's great talons and its wingspan of over twelve cubits, it could have carried Nell off if it wished. But Nell wasn't the delicacy it had in mind.

"Rrronk! Rrronk!" cried Minna, fluttering mightily as the great talons of the Skreek closed around her.

CHAPTER NINE

"Minna!" Nell cried, her heart pounding in terror. "Minnnaaa!"

"Pity," said Pim, peeking out from under a pepperberry bush. "She was such a nice little Dragon."

"Was?" Pim's words snapped Nell into action. "What do you mean, *was*? She's not dead yet. We have to save her!"

"Whoa, Princess," said Pim. "Like I said, she's a nice Dragon and all, but I haven't got any death wish. Do you know how many Imps have been killed by Skreeks?"

"Then you can stay here," said Nell. "Beauty, mount!"

Beauty lowered her head, and Nell whipped off the sidesaddle, hiked up her skirts, and mounted bareback.

"Away!" she cried.

"Wait up, will you?" Pim shouted, grabbing the tip of Beauty's tail as she lifted off.

Nell looked back. Pim was holding on for dear life as the great tail switched from side to side.

"I thought you didn't want to come!" she shouted.

"Can we . . . discuss that . . . later?" Pim yelled as he inched hand over hand up the tail to the Dragon's back, only to be nearly blown off by the wing draft. "Could you . . . possibly . . . lend a hand?"

Nell leaned back as far as she could and reached out her arm. Pim inched forward again until he'd almost reached her hand. Another blast of wind shook him loose and he would have tumbled right off had Nell not lunged and grabbed him by the seat of his trousers. She brought him forward and set him down in the hollow of her hiked-up skirt. He just lay there, his chest heaving, his face drenched in sweat.

Meanwhile Beauty was closing in on the Skreek. An arrow of pain plunged deep into Nell's heart when she saw Minna. The little Demidragon hung limp and apparently lifeless from the great claws. A sob burst from Nell's lips.

"What's wrong?" Pim was on his feet again, looking up at Nell.

"Minna . . . she looks . . ."

Pim scrambled up Beauty's neck to her crown horn. "Dead," he said sadly. "She looks dead."

He turned around and looked at Nell. "Sorry, Princess," he said. "I guess we might as well give up the chase."

"No!" Nell shouted, tears streaming down her cheeks. "Never! Dead or alive, I'm *not* letting that beast have her. Fly, Beauty! Fly!"

Beauty was closing the distance between herself and the Skreek.

"Flame, Beauty! Flame!" Nell commanded.

As soon as Beauty was close enough, she opened her mouth and aimed a stream of flame at the Skreek's tail. Though Beauty was fast for a Dragon, she was nowhere near as nimble as the bird. The Skreek quickly dove out of range. Beauty dove after it. Then the skreek looped around, came up from underneath, and raked its sharp head spikes across Beauty's chest.

"Rrronnk!" screeched Beauty. Her body shuddered with pain, but her wings didn't miss a beat.

"Be careful!" shouted Pim. "He can cut her wide open if he hits her right."

"What are we going to do?" cried Nell.

"Turn back," shouted Pim, "before someone else gets hurt!"

"Never!" shouted Nell.

Pim shook his head in exasperation.

"He's coming up from underneath again!" Nell shouted.

"Can't *you* do anything?" Pim asked. "Your mother was quite a Witch. Didn't you inherit any of her power?"

Nell's eyes widened. The sleeping spell she'd practiced all night! She put the reins into one hand, leaned over Beauty's neck, and pointed at the Skreek.

"Fall asleep, soft and deep!" she shouted. "Close

your eyes against the sun. Do not wake till day is done!"

Nothing happened.

Nell bit her lip and stared hard at the Skreek, concentrating all her energy on the spell.

"Fall asleep, soft and deep," she repeated. "Close your eyes against the sun. Do not wake till day is done."

This time, the great bird's wings slowed a bit, but only for a few moments.

"You need more strength!" shouted Pim.

More strength! Nell gripped Beauty's back with her knees and let go of the reins altogether. With her free hand she pressed the pendant against her heart. It glowed warm, and she felt its power surge like a lightning bolt through her veins. She pointed at the Skreek once more.

"Fall asleep, soft and deep," she cried once again. "Close your eyes against the sun. Do not wake till day is done."

The great bird's wingbeats slowed and then stopped! Its head drooped and it started gliding in a slow spiral toward the ground.

"It worked!" Nell cried.

"Yahoo!" shouted Pim, but then he pointed. "But if it crashes—"

"Minna!" Nell realized. "She'll be dashed to bits!"

Nell grabbed the reins again and sent Beauty into a dive. They came up under the drifting bird, and Nell stared at the limp Demi.

"How do I get her loose?" she cried. "If I pull her, I might hurt her even more!"

Pim, who was still perched on Beauty's head, heaved a great sigh.

"Clearly you're determined to get me killed today," he said, "so we might as well get on with it. Go up above the beast again so I can drop down onto its back."

"What are you going to do?" asked Nell.

"I'm going to save your worm, even though it's probably dead already," said Pim. "Don't ask me why. I haven't got a clue."

Nell smiled thinly. "Thanks," she said.

"Don't mention it," said Pim sarcastically.

Nell carefully maneuvered Beauty into place above the great bird.

"All right. Lower me down as close as you can and let me go," said Pim, "then drop back underneath the bird and wait."

Nell grabbed Pim by the back of his collar, leaned over as far as she could, and released him.

"Be careful!" she cried as Pim made a soft landing on the bird's broad back.

"Oh, right!" yelled Pim. "*Now* she starts worrying about me."

Pim burrowed into the Skreek's feathers, and Nell guided Beauty back down below the drifting bird. Pim reappeared, clinging to one of the bird's great legs. He slowly pried the huge talons open one at a time.

Minna dangled lower and lower until at last she tumbled into Nell's waiting arms.

"Oh, Minna." Fresh tears sprang to Nell's eyes. The little Dragon was as limp as a rag.

"Um . . . aren't you forgetting someone?" Pim called.

Nell looked up. Pim was dangling precariously from one of the open talons.

"Oh!" Nell cried, reaching up to catch Pim just as his grip slipped.

"Thanks a lot," said Pim. "Now let's get out from under here. This bird's about to come down!"

"Fly, Beauty, Fly!" Nell shouted.

Beauty surged ahead, and Nell and Pim looked back just in time to see the skreek crash into the dust.

"Tsk, tsk, tsk," said Pim, shaking his head. "That bird's going to have *some* headache when he wakes up."

Chapter Ten

Beauty's wounds were superficial, but Minna was barely clinging to life, her small body torn and battered. Nell pressed the ruby pendant to the little Dragon's chest, but the Demi was too far gone even for Queen Alethia's Magic. Nell's only hope was to reach the Palace of Light as quickly as possible. She dropped the reins and let Beauty take the lead again. Surely they would have a Dragon Master at the palace. But . . . another flood of tears gushed down Nell's cheeks. Some wounds were too grave even for a Dragon Master to heal.

"Hey, Princess," said Pim gently. "She's got a lot of heart, this little one. She'll pull through."

Nell smiled through her tears, hoping against hope that Pim was right.

Beauty was flying quickly toward the mountains in the distance. Would the Dragon know how to find the palace itself? Last time Nell had reached it through the

Corridor of Temptations, leaving Beauty and Minna at the door. She didn't know how the Dragons had been brought into the palace. And when they had left, it had been by Magic. All Nell remembered was mounting Beauty and hearing the Imperial Wizard utter the magic words, "Spirits of the Ancient Ones, spirits of the Yet-to-Come, speed these travelers on their way. Bring them safely home this day."

Then there had been a great roaring and whirling, like traveling through a tunnel of wind. When it stopped, Nell had found herself in the familiar skies over Xandria.

"How much farther?" asked Pim. He was sitting beside Minna, holding her head in his lap.

"I don't know," said Nell. "How is she doing?"

"Well, she's still breathing," said Pim. "That's about all I can tell you."

Nell bit her lip.

Beauty was climbing now, up, up above the snow-capped mountain peaks. The air turned icy cold and Nell shivered. After awhile her teeth began to chatter.

"Are you c-cold?" she asked Pim.

"Not too bad," he said. "The folds of your skirt are blocking the wind."

"I—I thought this was th-the mountain range where the p-palace was," Nell stammered, "b-but I d-don't see any s-sign of it."

White-capped mountain peaks stretched far into the distance. Below, a group of peaks formed a circle with a small lake nestled like a blue bird's egg in their midst. Beauty began to descend.

"B-Beauty must be th-thirsty," said Nell. She's heading for that l-lake down there."

"Good idea," said Pim. "We could all use a drink. Maybe we can get some liquid into Minna, too."

Beauty dove down, down.

"By the Scepter!" Nell shrieked. "I think she's going to dive right in!"

Nell grabbed for the reins, but it was too late. The water was coming up too fast!

"Hold on!" Nell shouted.

They plunged into the water, only . . . it wasn't wet. It wasn't even water. They were still flying, and directly below was the shimmering Palace of Light!

"Holy, roly, poly!" shouted Pim.

Nell looked up. Above them the sky was clear and blue.

"What the . . . ?" she said wonderingly. "What happened to the water?"

Pim looked up too.

"It was an illusion," he said. "Look at *that*!" He pointed down again. "That *is* the Palace of Light! You *were* serious."

"Told you," said Nell.

Beauty landed on the palace grounds, just outside the stables.

"Stay here with Minna," Nell said to Pim. She carefully pulled her skirt out from under the wounded

Dragon. Then she slid down Beauty's back and ran to the stable doors.

"Hello," she cried, pounding on the heavy wood. "Hello! Is anybody here?"

There was no answer.

Strange, thought Nell. But there was no time to waste. She ran back to Beauty again.

"Mount, Beauty," she commanded.

Beauty lowered her head to the mounting position, moaning softly as she did so. Nell reached up and took Minna gently into her arms, then she helped Pim down.

"Good girl, my Beauty. At ease," she said.

The big Dragon straightened again, emitting another cry. It was obvious that her wounds, though not fatal, were painful.

"Poor Beauty," said Nell. "Can you wait here with her, Pim? I'll send someone to look after her as soon as I can."

Pim nodded. "Go ahead, Princess," he said. "I won't leave her until I'm sure she's being properly cared for."

"Thanks," said Nell. "That's a comfort." Then she turned and ran toward the palace, cradling Minna like a delicate piece of china in her arms.

CHAPTER ELEVEN

The great mirrored doors of the palace swung open, and a tall, graceful Sprite stood blinking in surprise at Nell. It was Zyphyra, the same spirited Sprite Nell had met on her earlier visit.

"You again?" said Zyphyra. "I thought we'd seen the last of you."

Nell usually enjoyed exchanging verbal barbs with Zyphyra, but today there were more pressing things on her mind.

"My Demi's hurt," she said, "badly." She leaned forward so Zyphyra could get a good look at the bundle in her arms.

"Oh!" Zyphyra winced. "That does look bad."

"Beauty's hurt, too, but not as badly," said Nell. "Where's your Dragon Master? I tried the stable, but there didn't seem to be anyone there."

"There isn't," said Zyphyra. "We don't have a

Dragon Master. We don't even have any Dragons. The Imperial Wizard never leaves the palace."

Nell was taken aback. "Never leaves the palace?" she said. "Then how can he know the circumstances of Eldearth?"

"He has his ways," said Zyphyra.

Nell frowned. Not very effective ways, it seemed. She looked down at Minna's battered body and her heart sank. "No Dragon Master," she fretted. "What do we do now?"

Zyphyra hesitated a moment, then she took Nell's hand.

"Come on," she said. "Maybe Lady Aurora can help."

Instantly they were flying through a prism of light. Colors flashed and flickered. Lights swirled and shimmered. Nell had forgotten just *how* amazing the palace was.

Soon they reached Lady Aurora's reception room. Zyphyra left Nell in the middle of the room and knocked lightly on the Grand Court Witch's chamber door. A few moments later the door opened and Lady Aurora walked though, her gossamer white hair billowing around her like mist. Her eyes widened on seeing Nell.

"Princess Arenelle!" she said. "What brings you back to us?"

"I came to see the Wizard again," said Nell, "but we met a Skreek along the way and both my Dragons were hurt. My Demi is in a bad way." She held Minna out.

"I'll go see about your other Dragon now," said Zyphyra, zipping out of the room.

Lady Aurora came forward and took Minna into her arms.

"Oh my," she said gravely. "I fear it may be too late."

"No!" cried Nell, putting her hands to her mouth. "Please don't say that. *Please!*"

Lady Aurora sighed deeply. "The Keeper might be able to help," she said, "but he is not well. Your last visit left him very dispirited."

Nell looked up. "*My* visit? Why?" she asked.

"Because you told him the truth, my child—that Eldearth is worse off now than when he came to power, a truth that is very painful for him to hear."

"But . . . I *had* to tell him," said Nell. "He left me no choice."

Lady Aurora nodded slowly. "Nonetheless," she said, "it has had a bad effect upon his health."

Nell hung her head. It was all going wrong. She had been so proud of herself for completing the quest. She had had such high hopes of becoming Imperial Wizard one day, of making a difference. She was making a difference all right—she was messing everything up! Beauty was hurt and Minna was dying, and now, because of her, the Imperial Wizard was failing faster than ever. Instead of thwarting the evil Graieconn, she was playing right into his hands!

"Perhaps I should just go home," she said quietly.

"Maybe I can get Minna back to Galen, our own Dragon Master."

Lady Aurora pressed two fingers against Minna's neck, then shook her head.

"There is no time," she said. "She is fading."

A sob burst from Nell's lips.

"Please," she cried. "We've got to do *something*."

Lady Aurora gazed at Nell with genuine compassion. "All right," she said, placing Minna carefully back in Nell's arms. "Come. We will try."

Through glittering corridors, Lady Aurora led the way to the scepter room. "Remember," she said. "If the Keeper touches the scepter, it will glow very brightly. You must not look—"

"Yes, I remember," Nell said impatiently. "Can we just go in, please?"

Lady Aurora withdrew her wand from her sleeve pocket and waved it in front of the jewel-encrusted doors. Slowly they swung open and Lady Aurora disappeared into the shaft of light that poured through. Nell followed.

"Keeper," said Lady Aurora.

Once Nell's eyes adjusted to the light, she saw the Imperial Wizard slouched upon his throne, his eyes closed. The scepter, in its stand by his side, glowed brightly, but not quite so brightly as Nell remembered.

"Keeper," Lady Aurora repeated, and the Wizard slowly raised his head and opened his eyes. When his gaze fell upon Nell, he frowned.

"Not this one again," he said. "I have not the energy to deal with her today."

"Keeper," said Lady Aurora. "She comes on a matter of some urgency. Her small Dragon is dying."

The Wizard shrugged. "What concern is that of mine?" he asked.

Before Lady Aurora could reply, Nell walked forward.

"Please," she said, holding Minna out. "Can't you help her? You're her only chance."

The Imperial Wizard looked down his nose at the little Dragon.

"Healing takes a great amount of energy," he said, "and I've little left. Why should I spend it on an insignificant creature?"

"She's not insignificant!" Nell protested. "If there is one thing I learned on my quest, it's that no living thing is insignificant!"

"Here, here!" said a voice behind her. "I'll second that."

Nell turned to see Pim standing, hands on hips, staring defiantly up at the Imperial Wizard.

The Imperial Wizard's frown deepened. "Who on Eldearth are you?" he demanded, "and how did you come here?"

"I'm with the young lady," said Pim, nodding toward Nell. "And she is *quite* a lady, in case you haven't noticed."

The Wizard sat back and brooded, fingering his long beard.

"All right," he grudgingly agreed. "Bring the beast forward."

Nell rushed up the crystal steps to the throne platform and laid Minna gently in the Imperial Wizard's lap.

"Now stand back," he said.

Nell bowed and backed quickly down the steps again.

The Wizard reached out toward the scepter.

"Look away," he warned.

Nell and Pim shielded their eyes. For a brief moment the light in the room flashed with blinding intensity. Nell heard Minna utter a small moan, then the light faded again.

"Lady Aurora," said the Wizard.

"Yes, Keeper?"

Nell looked back up at the throne. The Wizard held Minna out to Lady Aurora.

"I have done what I can," he said. "Bind her wounds and feed her a gruel of Unicorn's milk and ground lemonseed. Time will tell if she will survive."

Lady Aurora gave Nell an encouraging smile as she carried Minna from the room.

Nell bowed low to the Wizard. "Thank you," she said quietly.

"You are welcome," said the Wizard, slumping back onto his throne. "Now, leave me in peace."

Nell hesitated. Should she just go home and forget about her quest? But what if she really was the Chosen

One and she gave up? Then Graieconn would surely win and the scepter would be extinguished. She had come this far. She *had* to try.

"Keeper," she said nervously, "there is still the matter of the apprenticeship."

The Imperial Wizard arched an eyebrow.

"Have you the mantle?" he asked.

"Well . . . no," said Nell, "but—"

The Wizard raised his hand for silence. "Say no more," he said. "There is nothing to discuss."

"But . . . I almost had it," said Nell. "My father had agreed to bestow it upon me, but then . . ."

"Then what?" asked the Wizard.

Should she tell the truth? Might as well. The Wizard was bound to find out soon enough, anyway.

"He decided to give it to my twin brother," she said quietly.

"Your *brother*?" The Wizard's eyes lit up. "Where is this brother? Why has *he* not made the quest?"

"He was hidden away at birth," said Nell, "to protect him from those who would betray him to Graieconn. We have only just discovered his existence."

"Well, then!" The Wizard seemed instantly reinvigorated. He rose to his feet. "The mystery is solved. The Chosen One has been found!"

"Not exactly," said Nell.

"What?" The Wizard eyes bored into hers.

"His Charm Mark no more resembles a dove than mine does," said Nell, "and a seer told my mother that it was unclear which of her twins might fulfill the prophecy."

"Nonsense," said the Imperial Wizard, waving Nell's words away. "Everything has fallen into place. Surely the boy is the One. The confusion over the Charm Mark is a small matter, which will likely be cleared up in time."

"You didn't think it a small matter in my case," said Nell.

"Your case is different," said the Wizard.

"How?" asked Nell.

The Wizard glared. "You are a *girl*," he declared. "Surely you will make a fine Witch, but you are not meant be an Imperial Wizard!"

"But that's not fair," cried Nell.

The Wizard chuckled. "Fair?" he said. "It's never been about *fair*, my dear child, not from the very beginning. Is it fair that the mighty Galerinn had to sacrifice his life for Eldearth? Is it fair that Graieconn still lives, spreading evil and causing suffering? Is it fair that I should dedicate my life to this thankless job, only to be told I've been a failure?" The Wizard shook his head. "No," he muttered, "it's not about *fair*."

"Begging your pardon," said Pim. He had come forward and was standing at Nell's side.

"Pardon denied," said the Wizard, turning his back.

"Now just a flaming minute here!" Pim hollered. "Imperial Wizard or not, you have no right to be so rude."

The Wizard cast an amused glance over his shoulder at the Imp.

"I have the right to be anything I choose, *little* man," he said with a sneer.

"You know what, your imperialness?" Nell suddenly blurted. "I don't like you very much. In fact I don't like you at all. It's no wonder you've done such a poor job."

"And you know what I think?" Pim put in. "I think the reason you won't give the princess a chance is because you're afraid. You're afraid this little slip of a girl might do so well that she'll make you look even worse."

The Imperial Wizard whirled and glowered at Pim. "If you ever again speak to me in such a tone, I will turn you to stone and use you as a paperweight!" he barked. "And as for your accusations, they are completely groundless. I *did* give the princess a chance, and I hereby offer it again. I will accept her as apprentice when and *if* she comes before me wearing the Mantle of Trust."

Chapter Twelve

Evening was coming on by the time the travelers set down in the paddock of Castle Xandria the next day. The Wizard had declined to send them home by magic, claiming to be too weak. Nell thought it more likely he was still simmering over their heated exchange of words. If ever she did succeed in obtaining the apprenticeship, she would have her work cut out for her learning to tolerate the Wizard's trying ways.

Minna was still unconscious, her little body encased in a cocoon of bandages, but her pulse was stronger and her breathing less labored. Beauty seemed tired, but her wounds were healing nicely and she no longer appeared to be in pain. Zyphyra had cared well for the yearling during their night at the palace, putting a healing salve on her wounds, feeding her a nourishing dinner, and bedding her down in a stall filled with fragrant hay. Nell and Pim were weary, but happy that their return trip had been uneventful.

Nell looked at the glowing windows of the castle. Owen was likely home by now, basking in the radiance of their father's love, maybe even wearing the mantle already. The precious *son*. She gritted her teeth.

No sooner had Nell dismounted when Galen rushed out of the stable, his eyes flashing with anger.

"Where have you been, Princess?" he demanded. "Do you know how much trouble you have caused me?"

"I'm sorry," said Nell. And she was. All the trouble she had caused, all for naught. She handed Minna over to Galen.

"By the Scepter!" He gasped. "What happened to her?"

"Skreek attack," said Nell. "She's doing better, but she's still going to need a lot of healing."

Galen shook his head. "You're going to have *some* explaining to do when your father gets back," he said.

"Gets back?" said Nell. "Back from where?"

Galen cleared his throat.

"Lady Fidelia will tell you," he said.

"No," said Nell firmly. "I will know *now*."

Galen sighed. "I'm afraid there was an ambush," he said. "Several of our best Dragonguard were killed, and Lord Taman and the young boy were taken prisoner."

Nell's mouth fell open. "Am-Ambush," she stammered. "Who? Who did this?"

"Gworfs," said Galen. "A whole battalion of them."

Nell's insides turned to ice. Gworfs were fierce fighters with horned heads, pincerlike claws and natural

70

body armor so thick it couldn't be penetrated by a sword.

"Gworfs?" she said. "But they are . . ."

"In the service of Graieconn," said Galen, nodding grimly.

Dread grabbed Nell by the throat. Was this ambush just a coincidence, or had Graieconn already discovered Owen's true identity?

"Where is my father?" she asked.

"He led a rescue party out this morning, Princess."

"Headed where?" Nell asked.

"Odom," said Galen.

Nell shivered. Odom was the mountainous region to the north—the direction from which the Dark Lord's forces always came. It was thought that the caves of Odom led to the caverns of Darkearth.

"I have to go after them," said Nell.

"Oh, I don't think so, Princess," said Galen. "Your father would . . ."

"My father is not here," said Nell, "and neither is Lord Taman. Which means I'm in charge."

Galen smiled. "Nice try, Princess," he said, "but it's the Grand Court Witch who stands next in the chain of command, not the half-grown daughter."

"Half-grown daughter!" Nell put her hands on her hips. "Are you aware that this half-grown daughter may very well be the next Imperial Wizard?"

Galen chuckled. "Right, Princess," he said. "Now, if you'll excuse me, I've got to feed and look after your

Dragons." He took hold of Beauty's reins and led her toward the stable.

"Zow. You're almost as invisible to them as I am," said a voice.

Nell jumped.

"Oh! Pim," she said. "You startled me. I forgot you were still here."

"Hmmm," said Pim. "Am I that forgettable?"

"No, of course not," said Nell. "It's just that . . ." She stared off toward the distant mountains to the north. "I've got a lot on my mind."

"Is the boy he mentioned that long-lost brother you were talking about back at the palace?"

Nell nodded slowly.

"So, it looks like maybe you'll get your wish after all," said Pim. "If the boy's out of the picture—"

"Don't *say* that," Nell interrupted. Her heart was thumping. "He isn't out of the picture. He *can't* be!"

"But I thought *you* wanted to be Imperial Wizard," said Pim.

"Not *that* way," said Nell, with a surprising rush of emotion. "We've got to save him, Pim!"

Pim arched an eyebrow. "We?" he said. "He's not *my* long-lost brother."

Nell sighed.

"You're right," she said. "This is not your affair—"

"Ha!" shouted Pim. "Just kidding! I've had more excitement in the last two days than in the last hundred years. I'm sticking with you, Princess, as long as you want me around." He did a little jig in the dirt, and Nell grinned.

"Thanks, Pim," she said.

Lady Fidelia bustled into the dining room.

"Oh, Princess, thank the Scepter you're back! I was worried sick. Have you heard the news?"

Nell nodded and put down her fork.

"Yes," she said. "Do you know anything more than Galen told me?"

"No," said Lady Fidelia. "Only that there was an ambush and Lord Taman and Owen were taken prisoner."

"Did the Gworfs give any indication that they knew who Owen was?" Nell asked.

"No," said Lady Fidelia, "but I am terrified that they might. They're not known to take prisoners."

Nell swallowed hard. "Then they'll be taking him straight to Graieconn."

Lady Fidelia nodded, her eyes flooding with tears. "Yes. I fear we'll never get him back, and I fear also for your father and his army. They don't stand a chance against the legions of Darkearth."

Nell turned to Pim, who was seated on a thimble on the table. "We have to beat my father to Odom," she said.

"How?" said Pim. "The army has quite a head start."

"Yes, but the bulk of the army travels on foot," Nell reminded him. "There aren't enough Dragons in all

Eldearth to accommodate an army. The Dragonguard travel with the army, acting as scouts and lookouts, and providing support when needed, but the army can only move as fast as the foot soldiers can march. With Beauty's speed we should be able to outdistance them easily."

"Who are you talking to?" asked Lady Fidelia.

"My friend, Pim," said Nell.

"Princess," said Lady Fidelia, "there is no one—"

"Yes there *is*," Nell declared. "Open your eyes, Lady Fidelia!"

Lady Fidelia leaned close over the table.

Pim stood up and put his hands on his hips.

"BOO!" he shouted at the top of his lungs.

"Aagh!" shrieked Lady Fidelia, clutching her chest. "There is something there!"

"Some *one*! Some *one*!" shouted Pim. "I'm an Imp, I'll have you know."

"An Imp?" said Lady Fidelia, blinking in disbelief. "I didn't think there were any Imps left in Xandria."

"Yes, well, that's quite *convenient* for the Xandrian to believe, isn't it?" said Pim.

"I'm . . . not sure what you're getting at, sir," said Lady Fidelia.

"We can have this discussion at another time," Nell interrupted. "Right now, Pim and I have to get going."

"Going where?" asked Lady Fidelia.

"To Odom," said Nell.

Chapter Thirteen

Galen's eyes popped when Nell walked into the stable toting her small sack of necessities.

"What on Eldearth have you got on?" he asked.

"Trousers," said Nell.

"I can see that," said Galen, "but why? And where did you get them?"

"Let's just say I got them from a long-lost relative," said Nell. "And as for why . . ."

"The princess is riding to join her father," said Lady Fidelia, sweeping into the stable with an air of authority. "Please prepare her white Dragon, Galen."

Galen's chin nearly hit the stable floor.

"Pardon me, Lady Fidelia," he said, "but I fear the princess has somehow bewitched you. She has rearranged the words coming out of your mouth so that it sounds like you are saying 'Prepare the white Dragon. The princess is riding to join her father.'"

"No, Galen," said Lady Fidelia somberly. "I am not bewitched. Those were my words."

Galen shook his head. "Have you taken leave of your senses?" he asked. "King Einar and his army left early enough to get through the Hill Lands before dark. If the Princess leaves now, she'll run smack into the Night Things!"

A chill zipped up Nell's back. *The Night Things.* She had forgotten about the Night Things. She took a deep breath to steady her nerves. "That can't be helped," she said, stepping forward and trying to act a lot braver than she felt. "Time is of the essence."

"Time for what?" asked Galen.

"Never mind," said Nell. "Just please prepare Beauty and give me a regular saddle, not one of those silly side things."

Galen sucked in a deep breath. "Well, I'm going with you, then. I'm not letting you go alone."

"I'm *not* going alone," said Nell. "I'm going with Pim."

"Who's Pim?" asked Galen.

"He's . . . an Imp," Lady Fidelia put in.

"An Imp." Galen looked at Nell and Lady Fidelia like they were both daft. "Even if there were any Imps left in Xandria, how much help do you think a three inch tall . . . *OW!*" Galen jumped. "What the . . . ? *OW!*" he yelled again.

Nell looked down. Pim was stabbing Galen in the ankle with a needle-sharp piece of straw.

Galen bent down to rub his ankle, and Pim stared him fully in the face.

"Three inches tall is tall enough to trick you!" he shouted. "That was no dust cloud you flew through yesterday!"

Galen's eyes widened.

"Well I'll be," he said. "It *is* an Imp."

"Sure is," said Pim, crossing his arms defiantly in front of his chest.

"Galen," said Nell. "I've *got* to get going!"

Galen straightened.

"Well, Imp or no Imp," he said, "I'm going with you."

"No," said Nell. "I need you to stay here and tend Minna. How is she doing?"

Galen grimaced. "She's not out of the woods," he said. "The next forty-eight hours are critical."

"All the more reason for you to stay," said Nell. "You've *got* to pull her through, Galen. You're the only one who can."

Galen nodded reluctantly. "All right," he said. Then he gave Nell a quizzical look. "By the way," he added. "Whenever I'm near her, I keep hearing a little girl crying."

Nell's eyes flew open.

"Raechel!" she said. "She must be trying to call Minna through the speaking star I gave her!"

Nell rushed over to the corncrib where the little Dragon lay.

"Arenelle, what . . . ?" Lady Fidelia began.

"Shhh!" said Nell, putting a finger to her lips. She

bent near Minna and listened closely. Then she heard it—a faint little hiccupping sob. .

"Raechel?" she said softly. "Raechel? Is that you?"

"Yes, miss," came the small voice.

"What's wrong, Raechel?" Nell asked. "Why are you crying?"

"It's the little Dragon, miss," said Raechel. "Is she . . . ?"

"No, Raechel," said Nell gently. "She isn't dead. She's hurt very badly, but we're taking good care of her. We're going to make her better."

"Oh, I'm glad, miss," said the little voice. "I'm awful glad."

"How are you, Raechel?" Nell asked.

"The Bloodpox is getting worse, miss," Raechel answered, "but I'm not afraid anymore. With this star I be able to see my mother and talk to her everyday. She even sings me lullabies at night."

Tears sprang to Nell's eyes.

"I'm glad, Raechel," she said.

"I'll never forget you, miss," said Raechel.

"Nor I you," said Nell hoarsely. She cleared her throat. "I have to go away for a while, Raechel," she said. "Will you do me a favor and check in on Minna now and then?"

"I will, miss," said Raechel.

"Good-bye, Raechel," said Nell.

"Good-bye, miss."

Lady Fidelia walked to Nell's side.

"Who was that?" she asked.

"A child I met on my quest," Nell explained. "She's afflicted with the Bloodpox."

"The Bloodpox!" Lady Fidelia said, gasping. "Oh my. She didn't cough or sneeze on you, did she?"

"No," Nell assured her.

"Did she even breathe on you?" Lady Fidelia asked.

"NO," said Nell. "Not really. She just gave me a quick hug and ran off."

"Have you any sign of a rash?" asked Lady Fidelia.

"None," said Nell.

"You're sure?"

"Quite sure."

"Well, that's a good sign," said Lady Fidelia with a sigh of relief. "The rash almost always appears within twenty-four hours, but keep a sharp eye out anyway. If you see any sign of a rash, I'll give you some Bloodpox potion."

"I knew there was a potion!" said Nell excitedly. "You must send some to Azwan right away."

Lady Fidelia shook her head. "I cannot do that," she said. "We only keep a very small supply on hand in case someone in Xandria is exposed."

"But why?" asked Nell. "Why not make more potion and cure all the Bloodpox on Eldearth?"

"The potion is made from the horn of the rare white Unicorn," said Lady Fidelia. "It's very difficult and expensive to create."

"But Folk are dying," said Nell. "Surely that justifies any effort and expense."

"I'm afraid these things are more complicated than you know," said Lady Fidelia.

"But Raechel *has* Bloodpox," said Nell. "She needs the potion."

Lady Fidelia shook her head. "It is not within my power to make such a decision," she said. "You must discuss this with your father."

"But you're in charge when he isn't here," said Nell.

"I'm sorry, Arenelle," said Lady Fidelia. "I know what your father's choice would be. He would not give our potion away and put our Folk at risk."

"But what of the Azwan Folk?" asked Nell. "Don't their lives matter as much as ours?"

Lady Fidelia sighed. "Of course their lives matter, Arenelle," she said. "But what if we gave away our potion and then we had an outbreak here? What if you were to come down with it, or your father?"

Nell swallowed hard. Could she even now be carrying the dread disease? What if she had passed it to her father, or Lady Fidelia . . . ?

"I don't know," Nell said quietly. "What is the right thing to do?"

"I don't know either," said Lady Fidelia. "I am glad such decisions do not fall upon my shoulders."

"Is this what Father meant," said Nell, "when he told me that as Imperial Wizard I would have to make hard choices and even cruel choices sometimes?"

Lady Fidelia nodded. "You are so young to carry such burdens," she said. "Still a child yourself."

"On the outside, maybe," said Nell. "On the inside I am growing older by the minute."

"Well, with age comes wisdom at least," said Lady Fidelia.

Nell smiled ruefully. "Not always, I'm afraid."

Galen came forward, leading Beauty. He had strapped her into a full suit of battle armor. In his other hand he carried a sword.

"No armor," said Nell. "It will slow Beauty down too much."

"But, Princess," Galen argued, "don't be foolish. If she is shot out of the air, her speed will be useless."

"That's a chance I'll have to take," said Nell.

Galen shook his head. "Well, you must take a weapon at least." He held up the sword.

Nell grimaced. "Even if I was inclined to carry it," she said, "I could never wield it. It's nearly as big as I am."

Galen sighed. "Well, it's the best I could find. We're not in the habit of sending half-grown girls off to battle."

"I can help with that," said Lady Fidelia. She pulled her wand out, waved it over the weapon, and mumbled a few words. Sparks flew, and the sword was reduced to just Nell's size.

"I still don't want it," said Nell. "I've got this." She pulled Owen's dagger from her belt.

"Surely you jest," said Galen. "That wouldn't hurt a flea."

"Well, neither would I," said Nell, "so it suits me perfectly."

"I, on the other hand, am a famous flea fighter," said Pim, "and I'd welcome a sword if you could shrink that one a bit more."

Lady Fidelia's wand was employed once again, and an Imp-size sword soon hung from Pim's hip.

Galen shook his head. "This is lunacy," he said.

"We've got to get going," said Nell. She transferred the contents of her sack—food, water, her speaking star, and warm cloaks for her and Pim—into Beauty's saddlebag. Then she led the Dragon outside and mounted.

Lady Fidelia gave Pim a hand up, then gazed at Nell with mingled fear and pride.

"Would that I had your courage," she said wistfully.

"Nonsense," said Nell. "I've seen your courage, Lady Fidelia, and it is formidable."

"Not like yours," said Lady Fidelia. "You are fearless."

Nell laughed. "Far from it," she said. "I simply do what I must, and I have no doubt that in my place you would do the same."

"You flatter me," said Lady Fidelia.

"I *know* you," Nell replied.

Lady Fidelia smiled. "Keep me informed of your progress by speaking star," she said.

"I will," Nell promised. She leaned forward and stroked Beauty's gleaming neck. "I hope you've had a good meal and a brief rest, my girl," she said. "We're off on another adventure."

Chapter Fourteen

The pale moon illuminated Beauty's scales, making her glow like a white paper lantern lit from the inside.

Nell peered worriedly into the darkness.

"Reminder to myself," she said out loud. "White Dragons are not the best choice for trying to sneak through foreign territory at night."

"So true," said Pim, clinging to Beauty's crown horn and pointing back over Nell's shoulder. "We've got company."

Nell turned to see what looked to be a flock of great black birds closing in on Beauty's tail.

"Night Things!" Nell shrieked. "Fly, Beauty, fly!"

But then there were more of them—on either side, ahead, above, and below.

"Flame, Beauty!" Nell cried, but it was too late. One of the Night Things had deftly tossed a noose around Beauty's nose and cinched it tightly. Another noose was thrown from the opposite side and cinched just as tightly. A third lassoed Beauty's tail.

"Rrriiii!" Beauty screeched through her locked jaws. She bucked and thrashed and it was all Nell and Pim could do to hold on.

The Night Things pulled their ropes and began forcing Beauty to the ground. Nell tried to reach into her belt for Owen's dagger, but before she could pull it free, a noose dropped over her head, cinched around her chest and pinned her arms to her sides.

"Pim, help me!" she cried.

Pim pulled his sword, but Nell was lurching so much in the saddle, he couldn't get a clean swipe at the rope.

"I can't chance it, Princess," he said. "If I miss, I could injure you."

"It's too late anyway," said Nell. Beauty was on the ground now. More and more ropes were tossed over them until Beauty was trussed like a fowl. There was no use resisting.

"At ease, Beauty. At ease," Nell called, fearful that the albino would injure herself with her wild thrashing.

Beauty ceased fighting, but her sides heaved and great shudders racked her body. She was clearly terrified.

Nell leaned in close to Beauty's neck, trying to speak in soothing tones. "It's all right, my Beauty," she crooned. "I won't let them hurt you."

Nell wished she possessed as much confidence as she pretended. Dozens and dozens of Night Things closed in around them. Nell had never seen a real Night Thing before, but from the stories of their hideous claws and great hairy bodies, she had made frightening pictures in her mind.

They looked nothing like she had imagined. They walked on two feet, like Tallfolk, and were actually Folk-like in appearance, except that they were covered with fur and had great wings sprouting from their shoulder blades. Their knifelike claws seemed to retract back under their skin when not in use. They had flat noses; small, straight mouths; and huge golden eyes that glowed in the night.

"Please," said Nell in a trembling voice, "we mean no harm."

The Night Things watched her curiously for a while, whispering among themselves. One of them finally stepped forward.

"You're a child," he said.

Nell was astonished. "You can talk," she blurted. "I mean . . . you speak Xandrish, just like me."

"You expected snarls and growls, I suppose," said the Night Thing sarcastically. "The truth is, we speak many languages. Why are you here?"

"I was . . . just passing through," said Nell.

"Passing through the Hill Lands at night is not allowed," said the Night Thing. He gestured to some of the other Night Things. "Throw her in prison," he said, "and let the Dragon go."

"Wait!" shouted Pim. "You're making a mistake."

The Night Thing squinted his eyes and came over for a closer look. "An Imp?" he said.

"Yes," said Pim. "Archibald Pim, at your service." He stuck out his hand, and to Nell's surprise, the Night Thing shook it.

"Donagh Treeleaper," said the Night Thing amiably, then he nodded his head toward Nell. "Since when do Imps cavort with the likes of these?" he asked.

"She's not like the others of her kingdom," said Pim. "I can vouch for her."

The Night Thing twisted his mouth into a sneer. "Ay?" he said. "I'll wager she wears her share of Montue."

Montue? Nell wondered. The cloak in her saddlebag was made from the lovely white fur of the Montue, a bearlike creature that inhabited the Hill Lands. All of her cloaks were Montue, in fact, but . . . why would the Night Things care?

"She doesn't understand," said Pim.

"Ay. I can believe *that*," said Donagh Treeleaper. "The Xandrian are famous for not understanding anything that might inconvenience them."

"I tell you, she's different," said Pim, "or I wouldn't be riding with her. The Xandrian have never been friends of mine."

Donagh Treeleaper gave Nell an appraising glance.

"What would you ask of me?" he inquired of Pim.

"Let her pass," said Pim. "I give you my word she means no harm."

Donagh considered. "I do not have the power to grant passage," he said, "but an Imp's word is honorable." He gestured once again to the other Night Things. "Bring the child," he said, "and stable the Dragon."

The Night Things cut Nell's bindings and helped her down from the saddle. Pim jumped to her shoulder.

"Where are they taking us?" Nell whispered as Donagh led the way through the darkness.

"To their village, I imagine," said Pim. "To see their king."

"Why didn't you tell me Imps were friendly with Night Things," Nell asked.

"You didn't ask," said Pim. "And by the way, you won't make any points with them by calling them Night Things. They call themselves the Hillkin."

"Why do they hate the Xandrian?" Nell whispered.

"Same reason a lot of other Folk dislike the Xandrian," Pim replied. "The Xandrian tend to act like they're the *only* Folk that matter."

Nell sighed. Eldearth was a far more complicated place than she had ever imagined while growing up behind the sheltering walls of the castle.

Donagh led the way up a steep hill and into a small cave. A few cubits in, the cave opened up and Nell blinked in surprise. She found herself in a beautiful underground cavern, lit only by the flickering light of hundreds of cook fires. Thin plumes of smoke rose up from the fires, escaping through open niches high in the vaulted ceiling. Great sparkling stalactites hung from the underside of the dome, giving the cavern the hallowed feel of a cathedral. Tiers of clay houses were built into the side walls and connected by graceful arched footbridges to other freestanding buildings. Villagers milled about the streets and walkways, conducting their business much like the villagers back in Xandria. It was all so . . . civilized. Nell never would have dreamed it. She had always imagined the Night Things as savage beasts, living like wild animals.

In the center of the cavern was a larger building shaped like a cluster of cylinders, all with conical roofs that flared out at the bottom, like pointed caps. It was to this building that Donagh led the captives.

"Wait here," he said, and he disappeared through an arched doorway.

As Nell waited, she became aware of a low moaning sound. "Do you hear that?" she whispered to Pim.

"Yes," Pim replied. "Sounds like someone in pain."

Just then Donagh returned. "The premier will see you," he said.

Chapter Fifteen

Nell and Pim were ushered through the door into complete darkness. As the others crowded in behind her, Nell was thrust forward, tripping over something and nearly falling.

"Forgive me," said Donagh. "I forget that you are as helpless in the dark as we are in the light." He called to one of the Hillkin near the door to fetch a torch.

"Thank you," said Nell, when the torch was brought in.

Donagh nodded. "Would that there were a torch that cast darkness in the light," he said wistfully. "Then you Xandrian would have a harder time of it."

"A harder time of what?" asked Nell.

"Stealing the Montue," said Donagh.

"Stealing?" said Nell. "The Xandrian don't steal."

Donagh threw his head back and laughed.

"I told you she didn't understand," said Pim.

"Ay," said Donagh. "Well, perhaps it is time we enlightened her."

89

"What does he mean?" Nell whispered.

"Look and listen," said Pim. "I think you're about to get a lesson."

By the light of the torch Nell could see that they had entered a large, circular meeting room. The floor was tiled with brick and the walls were painted in earth tones, depicting a life-size herd of Montue galloping in an unbroken ring. Rows of hewn log benches radiated out from the walls, leaving a circle of bare floor in the center. This circle was split by an aisle that ran from the doorway behind Nell to a similar doorway across the room.

The moaning sound—or more like wailing—was louder here and seemed to come from behind the door on the far side of the room.

"Sit," said Donagh, pointing to one of the centermost benches.

Nell did as she was commanded, and the other Hillkin crowded onto the remaining benches. Donagh knocked on the inner door, and a short time later it opened. The premier walked through, quickly closing the door behind him again, but not before a loud wail squeezed out. If any of the Hillkin were concerned about the sound, they gave no sign.

"All rise," said Donagh as the premier made his way to the center of the room. The premier looked very much like the other Hillkin except that he wore a cape of pure white Montue. He stopped before Nell and she bowed respectfully. To her surprise, he bowed in return, first to her, and then to Pim, who was standing on the bench beside her.

"I welcome you to Underhill," he said, "home of the Hillkin."

"Thank you," Nell and Pim replied.

"Captain Treeleaper informs me that you seek night passage through the Hill Lands," said the premier.

"Yes, Majesty," Nell began.

"I am not a 'majesty,'" the premier interrupted, "just a simple servant of my people. You may address me as 'sir,' as you would address any gentleman."

"Y-Yes . . . sir," Nell stammered.

"You seem surprised," said the premier.

"Yes, sir," said Nell. "It's just that you seem so . . . Xandrian."

"Ahem," warned Pim.

The premier's eyes narrowed. "Xandrian?" he said. "Are you calling me cruel, wasteful, and thoughtless?"

"Oh, no!" Nell blinked. "I meant that you are so mannerly and . . . and well-spoken."

"Hmmph," said the premier. "Obviously we have differing opinions of the Xandrian."

There was another wail from beyond the closed door, and the premier's eyes flickered in its direction momentarily. A shadow of worry darkened his eyes.

"Now then," he said shortly. "To what end do you seek this safe passage?"

"To rescue my brother, sir," said Nell. "He has been captured, and we believe he is being taken to Lord Graieconn."

"So?" said the premier.

"So!" Nell's eyes popped. "Lord Graieconn is evil, the Lord of Darkness!"

"Evil is as evil does," said the premier, "and darkness has nothing to do with it."

"How can you say that?" asked Nell.

"I can say it because Hillkin are people of the darkness, and there is nothing evil about us."

"But you raid our villages, carrying off livestock and killing babies," said Nell.

A gale of laughter broke out in the room.

"Killing babies?" said Pim, tugging on Nell's shirt. "Where'd you get that one?"

"Your ignorance is shameful," said the premier. "It is the Xandrian who are baby killers, and as for the livestock, you leave us little choice. You raid our lands by day, slaughtering our sacred Montue, taking nothing but their fur and leaving their carcasses to rot in the sun. The Hillkin used to be a proud, independent people, hunting the sacred Montue to feed our bellies, warm our beds, and clothe our bodies. Thanks to the Xandrian we must go naked now and sleep without warmth or comfort. To feed ourselves we have been reduced to stealing and making bargains with Graieconn."

"But . . . Graieconn is evil," Nell repeated weakly. "He would extinguish the light."

"And the Hillkin would have the upper hand over the Xandrian for once," said the premier. "That does not seem so evil to us."

"Ayyyy!" came a loud, plaintive cry from beyond the closed door.

The premier's head swiveled.

"Is there . . . something wrong?" asked Nell.

"No," snapped the premier.

"Ayyyy!" came the cry again, louder and more anguished.

The premier glanced around the room apologetically.

"You must forgive my wife," he said haltingly. "She is . . . not as strong as one might wish."

"Is she ill?" asked Nell.

"No," said the premier.

"Ayyyy!"

The premier winced.

"Please, sir," said Nell, glancing uncomfortably at the door. "She sounds like she's in pain."

"That is none of your affair," the premier declared.

Nell put her hands on her hips. "What manner of creature do you take me for?" she retorted. "Do you think I can listen to another's pain and not care?"

The premier stared at her a long moment.

"She is not in pain," he said gravely. "She is grieving. Our son lays dying."

"Oh!" Nell put a hand to her mouth. "I'm so sorry. What happened?"

"He stepped on a Xandrian Montue trap," said the premier. "His foot was badly crushed, and now he has a blood infection."

"By the Scepter!" Nell whispered.

"It happens to a lot of their children," said Pim quietly.

Nell shuddered. "I feel so responsible," she said to the premier. "Can I see him?"

The premier shook his head. "There is nothing you can do. His body alone can fight this infection, and his strength is gone."

Nell clutched her chest, and felt her mother's pendant grow warm beneath her tunic. She reached in and pulled it out.

"Please," she said. "I . . . can't promise you anything, but I do have some healing powers."

An even louder wail emanated from behind the door. The premier's face blanched.

"All right," he said. "Come with me."

Chapter Sixteen

The little child lay on a low wooden platform, his foot heavily bandaged, his body wasted. His sunken eyes were closed and his small face was flushed with fever. His breathing was raspy and shallow. A healer stood over him, chanting softly and wafting incense through the air. On a stool in the corner sat the child's mother, rigid with worry, her facial fur darkened by tears.

"We have a visitor, Maia," said the premier. "She believes she can help."

Maia's eyes immediately lit with hope.

"I will try," said Nell. "I can't promise anything." She sat carefully on the edge of the platform and reached out to embrace the child.

"What are you doing?" challenged the healer.

"I'm just . . . going to hug him," said Nell.

"What is this . . . hug?" asked the premier.

"I'm going to wrap my arms around him and hold him close," said Nell.

The healer's eyes widened. "Hugging is not allowed," he said.

"Why?" asked Nell. "Blood infections aren't contagious."

"Hugging is never allowed," said the healer, "especially with a boy child."

Nell was astonished. "You don't hug your children?" she said. "Ever?"

"Such displays of emotion promote weakness," said the healer.

"Weakness!" Nell frowned. "How can love promote weakness? Love is the strongest medicine there is!"

"This is our way," said the healer. "It is not for you to question."

Nell looked from the healer to the premier.

"Please," she said. "I don't mean to be disrespectful, but surely everyone longs to be touched, to feel love. It can only help."

The premier and the healer exchanged glances, then the premier looked over at his wife. Her eyes pleaded with him.

"Let the girl try," said the premier.

The healer scowled, but moved away.

"What is the child's name?" asked Nell.

"Ahava," said the mother, her lips caressing the name as she spoke the word.

Nell positioned the pendant over her heart, then she reached her arms around Ahava and hugged his hot little body to her chest. The pendant began to pulse between them.

"Help him, Mother," she whispered. "Give him your strength."

Thump, thump, thump, went the pendant as Nell clutched the child tightly, but there was no response.

"Ahava," she whispered softly. "Ahava you must hang on. You must fight."

Still no response.

At last Nell laid the child down again.

"I'm not strong enough," she said sadly. "My mother isn't even strong enough."

A small sob escaped Maia's lips, and Nell looked over at her.

"But two mothers might be!" Nell said suddenly.

"What are you suggesting?" asked the premier.

But it was clear that Maia understood. She was already on her feet. Nell took the pendant off and draped it over Maia's head, then Maia sat on the platform and gathered her son in her arms. She held him tightly, kissing his fevered brow over and over.

"Ahava," she whispered. "Ahava, come back to me."

The premier gazed helplessly at his wife and son.

"A father's love is strong medicine, too," said Nell.

The premier glanced at her uncertainly.

"This is foolishness!" declared the healer. "The girl is giving you false hopes."

"No," said Nell. "I'm telling you, if anything can give him strength, love will."

"Leave us alone," the premier said quietly.

With a sigh, Nell rose to her feet.

"No," said the premier, "not you." He turned to the healer. "You."

"But, sir . . . ," the healer protested.

"Please," said the premier.

"Yes, sir," said the healer. He glared at Nell as he strode from the room.

Then to Nell's amazement the premier walked over and sat down behind Ahava. Awkwardly he placed his own arms around both the child and his mother.

Long moments went by. No one spoke. No one moved. The premier relaxed at last and hugged his family close, kissing the child's head. A tear slipped down his cheek, and then . . .

"He's sweating," whispered Maia. "He's sweating! The fever has broken!"

The premier handed Beauty's reins up to Nell.

"You have taught me much Arenelle of Xandria," he said.

"As you have taught me," said Nell.

Donagh Treeleaper smiled. "The Hillkin do not forget their friends," he said. He reached up and handed Nell a slender piece of reed.

"What is this?" asked Nell.

"It's a whistle," said Donagh, "that only the Hillkin

can hear. If ever you're afraid in the dark, give it a blow and Captain Treeleaper will be at your service." He bowed low.

"Thank you," said Nell, tucking the whistle into her belt alongside Owen's dagger.

"I told you she was different!" shouted Pim from atop Beauty's head.

"Ay," said Donagh. "You were right, my friend."

Nell smiled. "I am ashamed of the way the Xandrian have treated our neighbors, the Hillkin," she said. "There is no reason why Folk of the dark and Folk of the light cannot live in harmony. I will speak with my father about changing things when I return home."

"Change is not always as easy to affect as one might think, Princess," said the premier, "but we thank you for your good will."

"I give you more than good will," said Nell. "I give you my word."

The premier nodded. "Go in peace, Princess," he said. "May your mission have a fruitful end."

"Thank you," said Nell. She stared grimly into the night. "How far is it to Odom?" she asked.

"The Hillkin can make it in a couple of hours," said Donagh, "but a Dragon will take longer. If you fly non-stop, you can probably reach the caves by midmorning, but I wouldn't recommend it."

"Why?" asked Nell.

"You'll need your wits about you when you start your descent," said Donagh. "You'd be well advised to get some rest first. Between the Hill Lands and Odom lies a broad plateau known as Graieconn's Footstool. You will be fairly safe there in the daylight."

Nell nodded. "Ready, Pim?" she asked.

"Ay, ay, Princess."

"Away, Beauty!" Nell cried. Then she shivered. "To Odom!"

CHAPTER SEVENTEEN

"Look! Up ahead!" Nell shouted after they had been flying hard for some time.

"Looks like an army," said Pim.

"Looks like two armies!" cried Nell, "engaged in battle!" Her heart began to pound. "Oh, Pim. One of them is Father's. I fear to look. How do they fare?" She swooped in as close as she dared to the tumultuous scene. Soldiers swarmed over the plateau like ants. Xandrian Dragonguard circled just above the fray, showering arrows down into the melee. The sounds of battle rose up on the wind—clashing swords, screaming Dragons, shouts and grunts, and worst of all, the cries of the injured and dying.

"They look to be holding their own," Pim declared.

"Is it the Gworfs they have overtaken?" Nell asked.

"No," said Pim. "I see no Gworfs among them. They appear to be Oggles, probably setting out from Odom for a night's pillaging when they ran into your father."

Nell shivered. Oggles were lizardlike Folk that could walk on two legs, or run on all fours. They had razor-sharp fangs, hawklike talons, and a taste for the flesh of Folk, dead or alive.

"Do you think Father needs our help?" Nell asked.

"No," said Pim. "By the look of it, he's got the upper hand. If you truly want to get to Odom before he does, this looks like a good chance to slip by unnoticed."

"I suppose you're right," said Nell, "but I do hope Father is all right." She glanced apprehensively at the battlefield as it zoomed by below. So many bodies lay strewn about, both Oggle and Xandrian. Her heart lurched. Could one of them be her father? She reached for the comfort of her pendant. "Watch over him, Mother," she whispered. "He is difficult at times, but I love him so."

"Explain something to me, Princess," said Pim, once the sounds of the battle had died away. "If Lady Fidelia doesn't think that your father's army can rescue your brother and Lord Taman, how are the two of us going to do it?"

"Three of us," said Nell. "We've got Beauty, too, don't we, girl?"

"Grummm," hummed Beauty.

"All right then, how are the *three* of us going to do it?" asked Pim.

"I haven't figured that out yet," said Nell.

"Oh swell," said Pim. "That gives me a lot of confidence."

Nell sighed. "Why is Eldearth so full of anger and hate, Pim?"

"Well, I'm no philosopher," Pim replied, "but most Folk say it goes back to the beginning, to the feud between Graieconn and Galerinn. I guess that's as good an explanation as any."

"It's not a reason for Folk to go on fighting and hating forever," said Nell. "There has to be a better way."

"Well, I sure hope you find it, Princess," said Pim. "It's nice to know someone's looking for a way, at least."

The eastern sky grew pale with the approach of dawn, but instead of the warm face of the sun, morning brought a blustery wind and a cold drizzle that pelted Nell in the face like tiny needle pricks. Pim ducked under one of Beauty's ears for shelter.

"Bet you wish you were small as me about now, eh, Princess?" he said.

Nell pulled her cloak from her saddlebag and handed Pim his own. The rain grew heavier, plastering Nell's hair to her head and trickling cold rivulets down her back. Everything ached—her head, her back, her legs. Pim sang ballads of bravery to keep up their spirits as Beauty soared on uncomplaining. Slowly the line of forbidding black mountain peaks loomed larger and larger.

"We'd better put down here," said Nell at last. "We're nearly there and we all need a rest and some refreshment before we're ready to tackle Odom."

"You'll get no argument from me on that score," said Pim.

Nell carefully surveyed the gray landscape below for signs of danger. Seeing none, she guided Beauty down into a scruffy little hollow with a small stream meandering through it. She slid out of the saddle, then helped Pim down.

"Oh," she said, arching her back and stretching. "I didn't realize how tired and sore I was."

"You think you're tired and sore," said Pim. "Look at Beauty."

Beauty's head was sagging and her sides heaved.

"Poor Beauty," said Nell, forgetting her own weariness. She rubbed the albino's neck appreciatively. "You've been through so much."

"Grummm," Beauty purred softly, leaning into Nell's caress.

"You miss your little friend Minna, don't you?" said Nell.

The great lavender eyes blinked sadly.

"I miss her too," said Nell. "But she's going to be okay. We have to keep believing that."

"Grummm," Beauty agreed.

Nell opened Beauty's saddlebag and lifted out a bundle of food wrapped in a cloth napkin, and her waterskin. "Here, Pim," she said, putting it all down in the dry shelter of a large rock. "Help yourself. I'm going to see to Beauty."

Pim went to work setting out a meal as Nell led

Beauty down to the edge of the stream. Nell knelt, scooped a handful of the water, and touched it to her tongue. Thankfully it seemed pure and sweet. She took a big gulp then motioned Beauty to join her.

The yearling lowered her head and drank eagerly. Nell rose and looked around. The landscape in the shadows of the mountains was bleak and barren, ashy, gray dirt and rock with just a few scattered stands of scrubby brush. Nell worried about food for Beauty. There didn't look to be any likely sources of Dragon browse.

"Come on, girl," she said when Beauty was finally done drinking. "We'll share what food I've brought, though I fear it won't look like much to you."

Pim was trying in vain to keep things out of the rain. He had opened out the napkin and laid out half a dozen pieces of fruit, a large loaf of bread, and a thick wedge of cheese. With his little sword he sliced off pieces of each for himself, then Nell broke the remaining bread and gave the larger chunk to Beauty, along with most of the fruit.

"Eat slowly, my friends," she said. "I don't know when we'll dine again."

They all ate in silence, too exhausted to speak. When the meal was done, Pim and Beauty promptly fell asleep. Nell was tired, too, but she had promised to keep in touch with Lady Fidelia, and she wanted to see how Minna was doing. She pulled out her speaking star.

"Lady Fidelia," she said, "at Castle Xandria."

The star began to glow. Colors swirled and sparks flew, then Lady Fidelia appeared in its center. She was seated in the library, reading. Oh, how Nell longed to be there beside her.

"Lady Fidelia," she said softly.

Lady Fidelia's head jerked up, and the book slid from her lap.

"Oh Arenelle, thank the Scepter," she blurted. "Are you all right? I've been trying to occupy my mind, but I can think of nothing else."

"I'm fine," said Nell. "Have you heard from father?"

"Yes, he is wounded, but not seriously. They had a nasty run-in with a battalion of Oggles."

"Yes, I know. We saw them," said Nell. "Pim said it looked like the Oggles were getting the worst of it."

"Yes, but not before doing a great deal of damage," said Lady Fidelia. "The army has been weakened considerably, and your father has had to send the Dragonguard to some of the other Tallfolk kingdoms for reinforcements. I pray there will be no further attacks before help arrives."

"I hope so, too," said Nell. "With luck maybe I can rescue Owen and get back to Father before there is any further bloodshed."

"Your father asked about you," said Lady Fidelia. "I didn't know what to say."

"What *did* you say?" asked Nell.

"I said that you were still adventuring," said Lady

Fidelia, "but that you had been in touch and you were all right."

"Good," said Nell, "and how is my little Minna?"

"Not much change yet, I fear, my lady."

"Oh." Nell's heart sank. She had so hoped for good news. "What does Galen say? He isn't giving up hope, is he?"

"No, no," said Lady Fidelia. "He continues to work his Magic. He said he will not give up while there is still a breath in her small body."

"Kiss her for me, Lady Fidelia," Nell begged. "Tell her how I love her, and beg her to keep fighting."

"I will, my lady. Now tell me please how you fare?"

"We are all well," said Nell. "Just tired. We are resting before we begin the descent into the caves."

"I am so worried," said Lady Fidelia. "I can't see how any of this will come to a good end."

Nell touched her mother's pendant, and it grew warm in her hand.

"There are forces at work that we don't understand," she said. "Have faith, Lady Fidelia."

"I will try," said Lady Fidelia. "I wish I were as brave as you."

"I am not brave," said Nell. "As I told you, I am simply doing what I must."

"There are many who would shrink from such responsibilities," said Lady Fidelia.

"I don't know how," said Nell.

"Ay," said Lady Fidelia, "and that is the difference."

"I must go now," said Nell, "and get some rest."

"May the scepter light your path," said Lady Fidelia.

The speaking star went dark, and Nell sighed. She stretched out on the soggy ground beside Beauty and closed her eyes.

"May the scepter light *all* of our paths," she murmured.

Chapter Eighteen

Nell's eyes fluttered open. Darkness was falling. How long had she been asleep? She looked over at Pim, still asleep in the shelter of the rock, using a breadcrumb for a pillow. Then she turned to look at Beauty.

"Pim!" she cried, leaping to her feet.

"Wh-What?" Pim sat up and looked around, bewildered.

"Beauty!" Nell screeched. "She's gone!"

Pim blinked and put a hand to his head. "All right, all right," he said. "Let a body wake up before you blast his eardrums out, please. She probably just went off to look for breakfast."

Nell's heart was thumping madly.

"Do you think so?" she asked.

"Sure," said Pim. "What else could have happened? Don't you think she would have raised a ruckus if anybody tried to steal her? We may have been tired, but we weren't sleeping *that* soundly. And there's no sign of a struggle."

"I suppose you're right," said Nell. "But where could she be? Beauty! Beauuuty!" she cried into the gathering gloom.

"Sheesh!" Pim stood up and put his hands over his ears. "Why don't you advertise that we're here? This isn't exactly friendly territory, you know."

"But I'm so worried," said Nell. "There's no sign of her."

"Why don't we just, oh, I don't know, *FOLLOW HER TRACKS?*" said Pim.

Nell looked at the ground and saw a fresh set of Dragon tracks leading away from the rock. "Oh," she said, feeling foolish. "Of course. I guess I just got so scared I wasn't thinking."

"Mmm," said Pim. He picked up his crumb pillow and took a bite.

"Time to get out of here anyway," he said. "It's getting dark and who knows *what* will be roaming around here any minute now. Thank goodness the rain has stopped at least."

Nell nodded. She left her cloak on the ground. It was soaked anyway. She shook the remaining crumbs from the napkin and tucked it inside her blouse, then she slung the waterskin over her shoulder. She gave Pim a hand up. He hopped onto the waterskin, then sat down and straddled it like a saddle.

"Away, Arenelle," he cried.

"Very funny," said Nell. She strode off, following the Dragon tracks.

"Beauty," she called softly.

There was no reply.

The tracks led up out of the hollow, along a ridge toward a small stand of scrubby bushes.

"I can't believe she'd wander off this far," said Nell after a time.

"She must have smelled food," said Pim. "Perhaps those are berry bushes up ahead."

But when they reached the bushes, there were no berries and no sign of the yearling.

"Look!" said Pim suddenly.

Nell whirled.

"What?"

Pim pointed through the tangled bushes to a small pile of charred sticks and ashes. Nell rushed over.

"A campfire," she said. "Someone's been here!"

"Yes," said Pim, pointing again. "Someone who seems to have befriended your Dragon."

Sure enough, two sets of tracks led out of the bushes—Beauty's and a smaller pair.

Nell's heart quickened. "Befriended?" she said. "You mean stolen!"

Pim examined the campsite thoughtfully. "I don't see any sign of a struggle," said Pim, "and those tracks don't look like they belong to anyone big enough to abduct a Dragon against its will. Still, it wouldn't be like Beauty to leave you and wander off with a stranger. My guess is, our friend is a Dragonsinger."

"A Dragonsinger?" said Nell. "What is a Dragonsinger?"

"A member of an ancient sect of Folk who can sing in a spellbinding pitch that is audible only to Dragons," said Pim. "Unfortunately Dragonsingers are a bunch of unsavory drifters for the most part, who turn their talents to profit by luring Dragons in and selling them."

"Selling them?" Nell stared at the two sets of tracks and swallowed hard. "But . . . those tracks are headed toward Odom."

"Exactly," said Pim. "Where our friend is hoping to make a quick sale, I'll wager."

"Oh, Pim," said Nell. "We've got to catch them! We can't let this . . . *creature* sell Beauty!"

"We'll try," said Pim, "but those ashes are already cool. They've got a good head start on us."

"Then we'll just have to move faster than them," said Nell, starting to run.

"Hey, hey!" cried Pim as the waterskin bumped and bounced against Nell's hip. "Take it easy, will you? A fellow could get killed this way!"

"Sorry," said Nell, slowing a bit and steadying the waterskin with her hand.

"That's better," said Pim. "You'll only tire yourself out running anyway. Slow and steady wins the race, remember."

"I can't afford slow," Nell replied, huffing as she hurried along. It was dark now, with just a sliver of a moon to illuminate the sky, and she had a hard time seeing more than a few cubits ahead. Beauty's tracks were deep and fresh, though, so the trail was easy to follow. It lead through a field of boulders and then started to wind up the mountainside. While Nell kept her eyes on the trail, Pim kept a watch out for danger.

"What's that smell?" asked Nell after awhile.

"My guess is it's the stench from the caverns of Darkearth," said Pim.

Nell's stomach clenched into a knot. "You mean you think we've reached Odom?" she asked.

"I think we're darn close," said Pim.

Nell sucked in a deep breath and threw her back into the climb. Up and up she went, rocks and pebbles slipping beneath her feet. There were places in the path that were so steep that she needed both hands and feet to climb. The tracks were no longer visible now on the rocky trail. Nell just kept moving steadily upward, hoping she was going in the right direction. She was growing tired and discouraged.

"We're making terrible time," she said. "At this rate father and the army may catch up with us before we reach Darkearth."

"And remind me," said Pim. "That is bad because . . . ?"

"Because they'll all be killed!" said Nell. "They're no match for the Dark Legions."

"And we are?" said Pim.

"No," said Nell, "but we're not going to fight them. We're going to outsmart them."

"Oh," said Pim. "Of course."

They had reached a plateau of some sort. The stench here was nearly overwhelming. Nell pinched her nose and stumbled forward, passing between two great, jagged rocks, then she gasped.

"By the Scepter," she whispered.

Pim stood up on the waterskin for a better look.

"Odom," he said quietly.

They were staring down into a deep chasm in the heart of the mountain. In its center was a bustling village, lit by torchlight and wreathed in smoke. A bedlam of raucous sounds echoed off the chasm walls, loud and wild even at this great distance.

"Beauty!" Nell suddenly cried. She pointed to a large, glowing white body making its way slowly down the mountainside.

"Hush!" Pim reminded her. "You're not back in Xandria, remember? You'd be wise to keep quiet and out of sight."

Nell huffed in frustration. "But if I could just call her," she replied.

"*Think*, Princess," Pim insisted. "If you call her, that bloke that's with her will instantly know we're here, and soon after, so will the whole village. Then what happens to your rescue plans?"

"But . . . it's so hard to be quiet," said Nell. "What if we don't reach her in time? What if he plans to hurt her?"

"If you ever hope to be Imperial Wizard, you'd better get used to making hard choices," said Pim.

Pim's words brought a little prickle of recognition.

"My father told me that once," said Nell softly. "He didn't think I'd have the strength to make those choices."

"Was he right?" asked Pim.

Nell swallowed hard.

"No," she said. Then she started down the mountainside, silently stealing from rock to rock, bush to bush.

Chapter Nineteen

By the time they reached the village, Beauty and her companion had been swallowed up in the crowds. The village was a tightly packed jumble of hovels, one shabbier than the next, some little more than piles of sticks. Tall torches, placed at intervals of twenty cubits or so, lighted the streets and lanes. They cast deep shadows among the huts, making it easy for Nell and Pim to sneak from hovel to hovel unnoticed. Nell had never—*could* never have—imagined a place like Odom. The streets teemed with the filthiest, foulest Folk she had ever encountered. They fought and cursed, shrieked and howled. They staggered down the streets smoking pipes and gulping joy juice. They jostled and jeered at one another, slobbering and spitting their words. Men . . . women . . . children . . . all dirty and smelly, with tangled, greasy hair and ragged, reeking clothes.

"Who *are* these creatures?" she whispered to Pim.

"Don't you know?" asked Pim in surprise. "The

Odomites are the cast-offs of Eldearth—the deaf, the dumb, the dim-witted, the deformed—the unfortunates that *proper* Folk have no use for."

Nell's eyes widened.

"You mean, they were regular Folk once?"

"They are regular Folk still," said Pim, "only they have grown up without love or law, raised by Graieconn's henchmen to be recruited into the service of the Dark Lord."

"Surely there are no Xandrian Folk here," Nell whispered.

"More than any other," said Pim.

Nell stomach turned over.

"But . . . how can this be? How do they come here?"

"They are cast out into the night when they are infants," said Pim. "The Hillkin take pity on them and carry them away, but the Hillkin, as you have seen, are barely able to feed themselves, so they are forced to bring them here."

Chills prickled the roots of Nell's hair.

"So that's what the Hillkin meant when they said that it was the Xandrian who were baby killers."

"Yes," said Pim. "It's a dirty business, and the Hillkin have no stomach for it, but the Xandrian leave them with little choice."

Nell shook her head. "I cannot believe this," she said. "You must be mistaken. Father would not allow such evil in Xandria."

"As the Hillkin told you," Pim reminded her, "evil is

as evil does. Each culture has its own definition. The Xandrian and many other Folk believe that Eldearth is better off without these Folk, that to allow them to live and breed would only weaken all Folk over time."

"And what do Imps believe?" asked Nell.

"Imps take care of their own," said Pim. "Many an imperfect Imp has proven to be a special gift to our people."

Nell shook her head. "How can I have grown up in such ignorance?" she asked sadly. "How can I have played with my toys and been content with my pretty things, never knowing or caring how others fared beyond the castle walls?"

"You are too hard on yourself," said Pim. "You are still a child, and you are learning."

Nell sighed. "I fear that if I live as long as you I will never learn enough," she said.

They were passing what appeared to be a tavern, filled to bursting with raucous, brawling patrons. A back door suddenly opened, and a young girl, not much older than Nell, came tumbling out. A pail of slop followed, bouncing off the girl's head and leaving a bloody gash.

"And don't come back till ya learns ta carry the slop pail proper!" roared a fat woman in an apron. She yanked the door shut again and left the girl sitting there looking dazed, with slop and blood dripping down her face.

"The poor thing," whispered Nell.

"You'd best not get involved," Pim whispered back.

"Don't be ridiculous," Nell replied. "She's hurt. She needs help."

Before Pim could say another word, Nell crept out of the shadows.

"Are you all right?" she whispered.

The girl jumped, startled.

"Who are you?" she asked fearfully.

"A friend," said Nell.

"I've got no friends," said the girl, shrinking back.

"You do now," said Nell. "Here. Let me help you." She pulled the napkin out of her blouse and poured some water from her waterskin onto it. She dabbed gently at the cut on the girl's face.

"Who are you?" the girl asked again.

"My friends call me Nell," Nell told her. "And this is Pim."

Pim stepped from the shadows.

"Hello there," he said.

The girl blinked. "An Imp?" she said.

"At your service," said Pim with a courtly bow.

The girl frowned. "Why are you two being so nice? What do you want from me?"

"We don't want anything," said Nell, wiping the slop from the girl's hair and face, "except to be sure you're all right."

The girl sighed. "Yes," she said. "I'm just stupid and clumsy, and that's why I'm always in trouble."

"You don't sound stupid to me," said Nell.

"I am," said the girl. "I keep making mistakes. I can't do anything right." She slowly got to her feet, and Nell could see that she had a hump on her back and one leg shorter than the other. She started to hobble off.

"Where are you going?" asked Nell.

"I've got to find me another job," said the girl. "Might as well just join the Rotters. They're all that'll have me."

"The Rotters?" said Nell.

"Those that work in the death mines of Darkearth," Pim explained.

"The death mines?" said Nell.

"Yes," said Pim. "Where they dig up the bodies Graieconn feeds to his Oggles."

Nell gasped. "You can't want to do that!" she said to the girl.

"Of course I don't *want* to do it," the girl replied. "But if I don't earn my keep I'll be killed, and I've failed at everything else."

"Princess," said Pim. "I think maybe we should . . ."

"Princess?" said the girl, looking skeptically at Nell. "You expect me to believe you're a princess?"

"Believe what you want," said Nell.

"What kind of princess wears trousers and skulks around in the shadows of Odom?" demanded the girl.

"I do," said Nell. "Arenelle, Princess of Xandria."

The girl's eyes narrowed. "Xandria," she said bitterly. "I was born in Xandria. I lived there until I was three, hidden away by my mother so the other Folk wouldn't see my deformity. But one day a peddler heard me laughing and peeked in our window."

"What happened?" asked Nell.

The girl snorted. "I'm here, aren't I?" she said. Then her eyes glazed over, and she stared at something beyond the mountains. "The hardest part was leaving my mother," she said softly. "I can still hear her cries the night they tore me from her arms."

Nell gulped, her stomach knotting in sorrow.

"Is . . . is your mother still alive?" she asked.

"I don't know," said the girl.

Nell pulled out her speaking star.

"Tell me her name," she asked.

CHAPTER TWENTY

The girl, Miette, and her mother, Matrika, could barely speak, both were so overcome with emotion. Nell took the star at last.

"Matrika," she said, "I am sorry that Miette was taken away from you. That was wrong. Terribly wrong, and one day I will change things if I can. My mission here is a dangerous one, so I cannot make you any promises, but *if* I return to Xandria, I will bring your daughter with me."

Matrika burst into tears again.

"Rrriii!" came a loud, piercing wail from somewhere in the distance.

Nell froze. "Beauty!" she whispered.

"Rrriii!" came the scream again.

"Who is Beauty?" asked Miette.

"My Dragon," said Nell. "A Dragonsinger stole her last night and brought her here."

An excited murmur passed through the crowded

streets of Odom, and the Odomites began to move in a great wave toward the center of the village.

"Ah," said Miette. "So that's why you're here."

"That's part of it," said Nell. "Can you help us find her?"

"Yes," said Miette. "I'm afraid that won't be hard. Just follow the crowd and you'll find her in the pit."

Nell's mouth went dry.

"A . . . a Dragon pit?" she stammered.

Miette nodded.

"Princess," said Pim. "I don't think it would be wise—"

"When have I ever done anything that was wise?" Nell snapped impatiently. "Let's go."

Miette bid her mother a tearful good-bye, then led the way through the shadows.

"This is crazy," Pim whispered to Nell. "You're just going to get yourself killed."

"Well, then, all my problems will be solved, won't they?" said Nell.

"Don't talk foolish," said Pim.

"*You* don't talk foolish," said Nell. "I can't leave Beauty in danger any more than I could leave you."

Pim sighed. "But it's impossible," he said.

"I don't believe in that word," said Nell. "If I did, I never would have gotten this far."

They had reached the village center. The Odomites were pushing and shoving their way into a large, rectangular building.

"Come." Miette gestured to Nell and Pim. "There's a loose board around back that the children sneak through."

Sure enough a small crowd of children were pushing and shoving one another in their rush to sneak through a hole in the side of the building.

"I can't fit through anymore," said Miette. "I'll wait here."

"You can wait with Miette if you want," Nell said to Pim. "I'm going in."

"Not on your life," said Pim. "I may think you're crazy, but we're a pair, remember? I've got to keep an eye on that hand I plan to ask for someday."

Nell chuckled. "All right, then," she said. "Keep your eyes open." She followed the last child through the crack.

It was hot and loud inside. Folk were shouting above the Dragon screams, placing bets and arguing with one another. The whole place reeked of unwashed bodies and stale Dragon dung. Nell pinched her nose and crept through a forest of legs until she came to a crude, wooden railing. It looked down into a deep stone pit, roofed over with a grid of iron bars. Two Dragons were chained to the opposite walls. One of them was Beauty.

Nell's heart broke to see Beauty's terror. Beauty thrashed and tore at the chain, her eyes white and wild. Flames erupted from her mouth, but the pit was too deep for any of the fire to reach the onlookers.

The other Dragon, a Red-crested, paced angrily, snorting and blowing. Occasionally it screamed, but it was more a scream of defiance than fear. Its numerous scars slowed it to be an experienced pit Dragon, and the fact that it was alive meant that it was a winner.

Pim had hopped up to Nell's shoulder. "Doesn't look like their flight muscles have been cut," he said.

"Thank the Scepter for that, at least," Nell whispered.

"You sure you want to watch this?" Pim asked.

Nell swallowed hard, her heart in her throat.

Beauty would be slaughtered. She was half the Red's size and was completely inexperienced in the pits.

Someone called for last bets, then a bell rang. Nell held her breath as the Dragons were released from their chains. In a fit of fury the Red flew across the cage, its great claws unsheathed, its fangs bared. Beauty huddled against the wall, staring, not moving, as if frozen in fear. Nell dreaded to watch, but then, at the last second, Beauty stepped aside and the Red crashed at full speed into the stone wall.

A gale of laughter swept through the crowd, and Nell allowed herself a small cry of exultation.

The Red recovered quickly and bellowed its rage. Beauty zipped across the cage, but the Red was right on her tail. He opened his mouth and blasted her with fire.

"Rrriii!" Beauty screamed, then she turned and met fire with fire. Both Dragons closed in, closer and closer, until neither could stand the heat and both turned away. In that instant, Beauty dove for the Red's neck, sinking her fangs into the unprotected area just under his chin.

A great roar went up from the crowd.

"Holy, roly, poly," whispered Pim. "She's holding her own!"

"Of course," whispered Nell wonderingly. "Why didn't I realize? She's had to fight all her life to survive, against whole packs of Dragons. One at a time is probably nothing to her!"

The great Red reared and shook his head violently, breaking Beauty's grip and flinging her hard against the stone wall. She crumpled to the ground momentarily, but then staggered to her feet and darted off. The Red gave chase, catching the tip of her tail in his teeth. Instead of trying to pull away, Beauty turned and flung herself into the Red's face, raking her claws across his eyes. With a scream of pain and fury he let her go. She darted off, but not before one of his huge claws slashed across her side, opening three parallel wounds. Beauty never faltered. She circled around and attacked again, digging her claws into the Red's back and biting hard into first one wing, then the other.

"She's got him now," whispered Pim. "She's paralyzed his flight muscles."

The crowd was going wild, some clapping and cheering, some shouting and jeering. Fist fights broke out, and soon there was almost as much violence in the stands as there was in the pit.

It all sickened Nell, especially seeing her gentle Beauty behaving like a raging beast, but she knew the yearling was in a fight for her life.

With the big Red grounded, Beauty took to the air, diving in time again with her claws and fangs bared.

The Red flamed and tried to fight back, but the albino was too agile, striking quickly then retreating time and again to the safety of the cage's ceiling. The Red sank at last to the floor, its great tongue lolling, its sides heaving.

The crowd was screaming, flushed with bloodlust now. "Kill! Kill! Kill!" they chanted.

"No," Nell whispered, closing her eyes and concentrating all her energy on sending Beauty a mind picture. "Mercy. Mercy. Mercy," she whispered.

Then a great hush fell over the crowd.

"Well, I'll be," whispered Pim.

When Nell opened her eyes, she saw that Beauty had fluttered down to the helpless Red's side and was tenderly licking his wounds.

CHAPTER TWENTY-ONE

As the crowd fought and rioted over dividing up the winnings, the iron grid of the cage ceiling was slowly lowered, forcing Beauty to stay on the ground. Then a great door slid open on one side of the Dragon cage. Handlers came through another small door and prodded Beauty with long spears until she fled, screaming in rage through the larger door and into a tunnel beyond.

"That tunnel must come up in a stable of some kind," whispered Pim. "Miette probably knows where it is."

Nell didn't wait to see what became of the Red. She crept back to the hole in the wall and out into the night. The air outside felt refreshingly cool, and though it still stank, it seemed sweet by comparison to the stench inside the pit barn. She took a deep breath.

"What happened?" whispered Miette.

"She won!" Nell replied.

"Wow," said Miette. "She must be some fighter."

"Not by choice," said Nell sadly.

"Do you know where the stable is?" asked Pim.

Miette pointed up the lane to a ramshackle building with a large, caged-in paddock area alongside.

"Doesn't look like it's very well used," said Nell.

"Folks around here don't get their hands on too many Dragons," said Miette. "Usually just Graieconn's broken down cast-offs, or misfits like your albino. That Red in there was an exception. His owner traded his wife to get her."

Nell's eyes popped. "His wife?" she said.

"Ay," said Miette. "She was blind, but there wasn't nothing else wrong with her, and she was a real beauty. Good thing she never saw what she married."

"But a wife isn't property," Nell protested. "What gave him the right to treat her that way?"

Miette laughed. "He was bigger and stronger. That's all the right a man needs around here."

Nell shuddered. "What manner of man would trade his wife for a Dragon?" she mumbled.

"Just about any man in Odom," said Miette. "Especially for a Dragon like that Red. He was a real champion. Your worm must be a champion too. The bloke that had the good sense to buy her made himself a pot of coin tonight!"

"Well, he'd better hold on to it," said Nell, "because he won't soon be fighting *my* Dragon again."

Miette bent low and led them toward the stable, hobbling from hut to hut through the shadows.

Nell could hear Beauty's angry cries now, and saw a torchlight flickering inside the stable. She ran ahead the last few cubits across a stretch of open ground, then flattened herself against the side of the stable. She crept toward the front until she came to a small square window, but it was too high for her to see through. She could hear voices, though, and loud laughter.

"Lift me up," whispered Pim. "I'll see what's going on."

Nell lifted Pim to the window ledge, and he rubbed a clear spot in the grimy glass.

"They're tending her wounds," he whispered. "She looks pretty tired out."

"I would imagine. The poor thing," Nell replied.

A loud gale of laughter broke out.

"They're sure celebrating," whispered Pim. "They're gulping joy juice like water."

"Good," said Nell. "I hope they drink themselves silly."

"They're trying to feed her now," said Pim, "but she won't eat."

Nell sighed. "I wish she would," she whispered. "She needs her strength."

"They've given up," said Pim. "They've bedded her down and doused the torch. They're . . . hide!"

Nell flattened herself against the wall again just as she heard a door bang open. Miette ducked behind a bush.

"Har, har, har," Nell heard someone laugh. "We got it made now, me friend. The womenz'll be fallin' all over uz tonight!"

Nell dropped to her knees, crawled to the corner of the stable, and cautiously peeked around. Two Odomites stood in front of the stable door. One was turning a key in a large padlock.

"That'll hold our li'l treasure," the man said, dropping the key into his jerkin pocket and patting it fondly. "She's gonna make us rich, ain't she, Dweeb?"

"Ar," said the one called Dweeb. He had a jug of joy juice hanging from one hand. "Lez go find uz some prettiez," he suggested.

The two walked off arm in arm, passing the jug back and forth between them.

As soon as they were out of sight, Nell looked left and right, then ran to the door. She grabbed the padlock and tugged, but it was large and strong. She threw herself against the door, but it was heavy and sound.

She heard a burst of raucous laughter and turned to see a group of Odomites coming toward her. Quickly she darted back around the stable and hid behind a bush.

"Hey," yelled Pim from the window ledge. "Aren't you forgetting someone!"

"Shush!" Nell warned.

The group staggered by, telling colorful jokes and guffawing loudly. Nell waited until they were gone from sight, then she popped up and reached for Pim.

"The stable is locked," she whispered, "and they took the key."

"Let's go have a look," said Pim.

Nell lifted him to her shoulder and crept back to the door again. Miette waited in the shadows, keeping watch.

"We're in luck," said Pim.

"How?" asked Nell.

"That keyhole is just my size," said Pim. "Give me a hand."

Nell lifted Pim to the keyhole and he disappeared inside. She heard a couple of metallic clicks and then the lock fell open. Pim stuck his head out and grinned.

"Do we make a good pair or what?" he asked.

Nell smiled. "We sure do," she said.

Pim climbed back onto her shoulder, then, after making sure the coast was still clear, Nell opened the door a crack and slipped inside. A moment later, Miette followed. The stable was almost completely dark, lit only by the outside torchlight flickering through the small windows.

"Beauty?" she whispered.

"Grummm," came a faint reply from the shadows.

Nell rushed toward the sound and fell to her knees by the Dragon's side.

"Oh, Beauty," she whispered, throwing her arms around the Dragon's neck and hugging her tight.

"Hey, careful there," said Pim. "I'm getting squished."

Nell pulled back and Pim jumped to Beauty's side.

"Rrronnk." Beauty moaned.

"Oh, Pim, be careful," whispered Nell. "She's hurt."

"Why . . . she's an albino," said Miette wonderingly.

"Yes," said Nell. "That's why she's such a fighter. She's had to fight all her life just to live."

"I know how *that* feels," said Miette quietly.

Nell's eyes were adjusting to the light. She could see where Beauty was crudely bandaged and other spots where she was singed and bruised.

"Poor Beauty," she whispered, stroking the albino's long, white neck. "I'm so sorry."

"She looks awfully weak," said Pim. "She's not going to be able to go any farther."

Nell bit her lip. "You're right, Pim," she said. "We've got to get her out of here and hide her somewhere."

"How?" asked Pim. "She's too weak to fly, and if we try and walk her out of here, they'll just follow her tracks."

"You don't know Beauty," said Nell. "I've seen her fly in worse shape than this."

Outside, the noise in the village was growing ever louder and more raucous. The Dragon fight had obviously sparked a huge celebration.

"I don't know," said Pim. "Even if she can fly, where are you going to take her?"

"I'm not taking her anywhere," said Nell. "You are."

"What?" cried Pim.

"I've got to keep going," said Nell. "You have to find someplace where she can rest."

"Oh no," said Pim. "You're not going anywhere without me. We're a pair, remember?"

"I'll take her," said Miette. "I know a place, a cave up on the mountain where I used to hide when I was a child."

"Can you fly a Dragon?" asked Nell.

"Until I met you," said Miette, "I didn't think I could do anything. Now I know I just never cared enough to try. I've got a reason to care now, thanks to you. I'll get your Dragon to safety."

"How will you get her out of here unseen?" Nell asked.

"That part's easy," said Miette. "Just listen to that celebration going on out there. The joy juice is taking effect. They'll be partying most of the night, then they'll fall into a sleep as deep as a spell."

Nell nodded. "Okay," she said. "Where do we find the cave when we get back?"

Miette took her to the window and pointed. "Up there," she said, "just above that ridge. That's where Beauty and I will be waiting."

Nell nodded. "All right," she said, then she reached for Pim.

"Where are we going?" asked Pim, once he'd settled himself into his usual seat on the waterskin.

Nell picked up a handful of hay and stuffed it into her shirt behind one shoulder, then she hitched her trousers to one side and tilted her hips to make herself look lame, like Miette.

"We're off to join the Rotters," she said.

Chapter Twenty-two

"All right, step lively there. Step lively!" the ghoulish guard ordered, growling.

The line of new recruits marched slowly down into the bowels of a stinking, stifling cave. Nell hobbled along, trying as much as possible to stay out of sight behind a great shuffling hulk of a man who sang a nonsensical tune to himself as they walked. One of the other Odomites had stolen her waterskin, so Pim rode on her shoulder now, hidden beneath her hair.

The cave opened out into a deep, cylindrical cavern, dimly lit by flickering torchlight. The path wound round and round its outer walls, spiraling down, down, down into deepening blackness. A vast network of caverns opened off this central one on many different levels. The caverns were strangely beautiful with tall columns of luminescent calcite that supported walkways and bridges. Colorful mineral deposits bloomed on the walls and floors, and chandelier-like stalagmites, intricately carved by nature, dripped from the chamber ceilings. Some levels seemed to contain housing, others industry or mining operations, and still others military training facilities. Ghouls, Gworfs, Oggles, Ogres . . . fearsome Deepdwellers of all kinds roamed throughout the complex. Nell willed herself to stay calm in their presence. If she gave in to her terror, she would never be able to continue with her mission. She pressed her hand against her chest, feeling her mother's ruby pendant beneath her blouse. Its warmth gave her strength.

"Nice neighborhood," whispered Pim as a trio of foul-smelling Ogres stopped to jeer and poke fun at the new recruits.

"What a sorry bunch," said one. "No wonder yer mothers didn't want ya."

"Arr," said another. "Thank your stars that the Dark Lord takes pity on yer worthless hides. If it were up to me, I'd let you starve."

"Ar, look at this one!" shouted the third. He pointed to the big man in front of Nell. "Body that size and a brain like a pea!"

The big man seemed to curl farther into himself with each nasty comment. His singing became louder and more rapid, as if he was trying to drown out the sounds of the Ogres' voices. His two hands, hanging limply on either side of his hulking body, began to tremble.

"What's wrong?" The first Ogre asked. "You deaf, too?" He reached out a hairy finger and poked the big man in the side.

The man just kept shuffling along, singing more and more loudly.

"Hey!" shouted the second Ogre. "We're talking to you!" He grabbed the man by the shirt and yanked him out of the line. The man was big enough to crush the Ogre with one fist if he'd wished, but obviously he was too childlike and timid. He began to shuffle from one foot to the other, twisting his hands together. He sang the same short phrase over and over. It sounded like, "Ock I weed yay yee. Ock I weed yay yee." Nell found the tune oddly familiar.

The Ogre pulled the man closer, leaned in and looked up at his face. "What are you singing?" he asked.

"Ock I weed yay yee," sang the man nervously.

"The poor man," Nell whispered to Pim. "Why don't they leave him alone?"

"Because they're so miserable themselves that their only pleasure is to make someone else even more miserable," Pim replied.

The third Ogre now shoved his face toward the big man's face, too. "Answer us!" he shouted. "What is that yer singing?"

"Ock I weed yay yee," the man repeated, tears slipping down his round cheeks now.

"Hey," whispered Nell. "I know what that song is. It's a Xandrain lullaby—'Rock my Sweet Baby'!"

"What's the hold-up here?" demanded the guard, walking back from the head of the line.

"This ugly beast insulted me," said the first Ogre.

"Yes," said the second. "He called 'im dungbreath."

"He did, did he?" said the guard, drawing his sword. "Let's see if he's so brash once he's lost an ear!"

The big man began to whimper.

The guard lifted his sword.

"No!" Nell cried.

"Shush!" Pim whispered in her ear.

"I will not," said Nell.

The guard and the Ogres turned their attention to her.

"You will not *what*?" demanded the guard.

"I will not stand here and allow you to hurt this poor man for no reason," said Nell.

The guard's eyes widened. "And just who are you?" he asked.

"I'm . . . I'm Mie . . . nod," said Nell, remembering at the last second that she was dressed as a boy, "and these three Ogres are lying. This man never spoke a word to any of them."

"I don't recall asking you to butt in," said the guard, "so butt out!"

He raised his sword again.

"Quiet, quiet, quiet!" whispered Pim, tugging on a lock of Nell's hair.

"No!" Nell cried. She jumped in front of the big man. "Leave him alone. Can't you see he's slow-witted. He's just singing a lullaby. He must remember it from when he was a baby. It's probably all he knows."

The guard eyed her critically.

"You're moving mighty fast all of a sudden," he said. "What happened to that gimp of yours?"

"Now you've done it!" hissed Pim.

"It . . . wasn't really a gimp," said Nell. "I just twisted my ankle awhile back. It's feeling better all of a sudden."

"Look who's calling us liars," said one of the Ogres.

"Ar," said the guard, narrowing his eyes and poking Nell in the chest. "Methinks you could use some time in the dungeon to refresh your memory." He looked up at the big man, who had begun softly singing again. "And since you seem so fond of dimwit here, you can share a cell with him for a while. See how much you like that lullaby of his once you've heard nothing else for days."

CHAPTER TWENTY-THREE

"That way," said the guard, pointing to a stone bridge that arched off to the right. He was about to prod the big man with his sword when Nell gently took the man's hand and pulled him after her onto the bridge.

"Come on, sweet baby," she said.

The man followed docilely.

"Watch for a chance to escape," Nell whispered to Pim.

"What was that you said?" asked the guard.

Nell cleared her throat.

"I . . . um . . . said I must have dropped my cape," she quipped.

"Ar, well ain't that too bad," said the guard. "Keep moving!"

The bridge led to the mouth of another cavern, dark and quiet. There was no hustle or bustle here, just a sinister-looking fortress, all jagged edges and sharp spires.

A moat of greasy-looking black water surrounded it, and in the water, serpents slithered. Nell's skin crawled.

The guard led them to the edge of the moat. "Prisoners, ho!" he yelled.

"No room," returned a surly voice from one of the tower windows.

"Make room!" shouted the guard.

"'Ow many?" growled the voice.

"Two," yelled the guard.

There was a long silence, then two muffled screams rang out, one after the other. Nell gulped, goose bumps breaking out all over her body.

"Maybe you'll listen next time I tell you to keep quiet," whispered Pim.

"Ock I weed ya yee," sang the big man softly.

Nell's heart raced. They had to escape—now! She couldn't face being locked up in that awful building.

"If you were to give that a guard a shove right now," Pim whispered, "those serpents down there would be mighty grateful."

Nell looked down into the moat and her stomach lurched. She couldn't. She just couldn't. Then she remembered something her father had said to her when she'd first discussed the Imperial Wizardry with him. *Your heart is too soft, Nell.*

Trembling, she took a step forward and lifted her hand.

Just then there was a metallic clunk, and across the moat a big drawbridge began to lower slowly.

"Too late!" whispered Pim.

The guard turned. "What are you doing?" he snapped.

Nell dropped her hand and stepped back.

"I . . . I was . . . just showing this man the draw-bridge," she stammered.

The guard glanced at the big man, then narrowed his eyes at Nell. "Watch your step, boy," he said, growling.

The drawbridge clanged into place and a door opened in the wall on the far side. A Gworf came out onto the bridge, dragging what looked like a body.

Splash! Nell heard, and then the moat water boiled. She closed her eyes. Moments later, there came a second splash.

"Any more funny business and you'll be next," the guard warned, giving Nell a jab in the ribs.

"Bring 'em in!" called the Gworf.

The guard took Nell and the big man across the moat and delivered them into the care of the Gworf.

"This way," the Gworf ordered, growling. He pushed Nell and the man ahead of him into the gloom of the building with his right claw. His left claw rested on the hilt of his sword.

Nell walked straight ahead down a dim, torch-lit cor-ridor, her heart in her throat. The big man shuffled along behind her, followed by the Gworf.

The building stank of rot and filth and worse. Low moans were heard from behind bolted doors on either side of the hall. Nell's stomach was in a knot. What had she gotten them into? She had tucked the dagger away out of sight in the waistband of her trousers. She reached up under her blouse, her hand closing around its hilt. Could she find the courage to use it?

"Forget it," Pim whispered, obviously guessing her intent. "He's a Gworf, remember? His skin is like iron."

Nell swallowed, secretly relieved that the choice had been made for her. But she had to come up with another idea, fast! A sleeping spell, perhaps? It was worth a try. She touched her mother's pendant, then turned and pointed at the Gworf, concentrating with all her strength.

"Fall asleep, soft and deep," she cried. "Close your eyes against the sun. Do not wake till day is done."

The Gworf stopped in his tracks and stared at her, then he threw his head back and laughed. "Sun?" he said. "What sun? Don't waste yer breath, boy. Yer fool-ish spell won't work on me." Then he sneered. "But it *will* git you a night in the dungeon."

"Nice going," whispered Pim.

Nell sighed. What else could go wrong?

"Through that door," said the Gworf when they reached the end of the corridor.

Nell pushed the door open and saw a circular stairway.

"Down," said the Gworf.

Nell began the descent, one flight of stairs, then another narrower flight. The big man followed close on her heels, still singing softly.

The stairs were damp and slimy, and rivulets of

water trickled down the stone walls. Crickets chirped and frogs croaked. Salamanders and centipedes scurried into the shadows. At the bottom of the stairs Nell stepped off into a puddle of fetid water. In front of her was a single, heavy door.

"'Ere we are," said the Gworf, grinning cruelly. "'Ome sweet 'ome."

He lifted an iron bar from across the door and pushed it open. It was pitch dark inside. Several frogs croaked.

"In you goes," he said.

Nell waded cautiously into the darkness, but the big man held back.

"Git in there," growled the Gworf, giving him a shove.

The man braced both hands against the doorframe and refused. "Dark," he said, staring into the blackness in wide-eyed terror.

"Git in or die!" yelled the Gworf, pulling his sword.

Nell reached back for the man's hand.

"Rock my sweet baby," she began to sing softly. "Rock, rock, my sweet baby child."

The man dropped his arms and quietly followed her into the room.

CLANG! banged the door behind them, shutting out the last ray of light.

"Well, it's about time!" came a voice from the gloom.

CHAPTER TWENTY-FOUR

Nell's mouth fell open.

"Owen!" she cried, gasping.

"Yes," said Owen shortly. "I thought you said that if I cooperated they wouldn't throw me in a dungeon!"

Nell blinked in confusion.

"What are you talking about?" she asked.

"You told me just play along with everything and you'd explain later," said Owen. "But this is a bit much, don't you think?"

Nell couldn't help laughing.

"You don't really think I had anything to do with you ending up here, do you?" she asked.

Owen huffed. "I don't know what to think," he said. "All I know is, I'm really starting to regret the day I ever set eyes on you."

"Ock I weed ya yee," sang the big man nervously.

"Huh?" said Owen. "Who's your big friend, and what is he talking about?"

"I don't know who he is," said Nell. "I just call him 'sweet baby.'"

"Why?" asked Owen.

"It's a long story."

"Ahem," said Pim. "Since you're making introductions . . ."

"Oh, I'm sorry," said Nell. "Owen, this is my friend Archibald Pim."

"I thought you just said you didn't know who he was?" said Owen in a confused voice.

"No," said Nell. "I don't know who Sweet Baby is. Pim is my friend."

"But . . . I only saw two Folk come through the door," said Owen.

"Pim was hiding in my hair," said Nell.

"Hiding . . . *where?*"

"Here," said Pim, "in her hair. I'm an Imp, you see."

"No, I don't see anything," said Owen. "It's pitch black in here."

"Well, if you could see," said Nell, "you'd see a three-inch tall man sitting on my shoulder."

"An oversized baby and an undersized man," said Owen. "Strange choice of traveling companions."

"Hey," said Pim. "Watch who you're calling undersized. I happen to be tall for an Imp, and I'll wager I'm a bigger *man* than you are."

"Oh, yeah, sounds like it," said Owen, "riding around hiding in a girl's hair."

"All right bud—," said Pim.

"Enough, you two!" said Nell. "We're all on the same side, remember? Let's try and concentrate on how we're going to get out of here."

"You mean . . . we really *are* prisoners?" asked Owen.

"Hmmph," snorted Pim. "Easy to see who got the brains in the family."

"What are you mumbling about now?" Owen growled.

"Never mind," said Nell. "Where's Lord Taman?"

"I don't know," said Owen. "Don't you know?"

"How would I know?" asked Nell.

Owen huffed. "Look," he said. "You told me *you* were going to explain everything, remember?"

"That was before the ambush," said Nell.

"But I thought the ambush was part of the whole thing," said Owen.

"Why would we stage an ambush?" asked Nell.

"I don't *know*," said Owen. "I don't know why you do any of the cloppin' crazy things you do."

"Hey, watch your mouth, kid," said Pim. "This here's a lady you're talking to."

"No, it's not," said Owen. "I wasn't talking to *you*."

"All right. That's it! Let me at him!" yelled Pim. He jumped to his feet.

"I said *enough*, you two!" Nell shouted.

Clunk, clunk, clunk, came the heavy thud of footsteps coming down the stairs. The iron bar locking the door was lifted and the door swung into the room. Silhouetted against the flickering torchlight were two figures—the Gworf and another person.

"Well, well," said a familiar voice. "Just look who we have here. How cozy."

"Lord Taman!" cried Nell, rushing forward. "Thank the Scepter! How did you get free?"

Lord Taman chuckled. "I've always been free, dear cousin," he said.

Nell stopped in her tracks. She looked from Lord Taman to the Gworf and back, a strange uneasiness beginning in her stomach.

"But you and Owen were taken prisoner," Nell went on.

"So it may have appeared," said Lord Taman, "but as you can see, the only prisoners in this room are you three."

Nell's blood turned to ice.

"But . . . but you're on our side. Just days ago you saved me from the Minister of Magic," she stammered.

"To throw you all off the track, of course," said Lord Taman with a droll smile.

"You mean . . . you're one them! One of the traitors!" Nell gasped.

"Tsk, tsk, tsk." Lord Taman clucked. "Such a nasty word. I'm nothing of the kind. I'm completely loyal . . . to Lord Graieconn! Now, out of my way. My lord would like a word with our young friend here."

"No!" cried Nell, putting her arms out to block Lord Taman.

"Come now, Arenelle," he said. "Don't be difficult." He shoved her roughly to one side and reached for Owen.

Owen retreated into the shadows at the back of the cell.

Nell regained her footing and rushed to Owen's side. She pressed the dagger into his hand, then turned and threw herself at Lord Taman.

"Get her off me!" Lord Taman yelled to the Gworf.

The Gworf strode into the room and grabbed Nell by the hair. He lifted her into his arms and started to squeeze.

"Let me go! Let me go!" she shrieked, flailing and kicking.

Lord Taman lunged at Owen and grabbed his hand.

"Come with me, you little brat," he yelled, "before I lose my temper!"

"Let me . . . ach." Nell coughed. The Gworf was squeezing the breath from her lungs.

"Ouch!" cried Lord Taman. He jumped back, lifting his hand up to the dim light. A ribbon of blood trickled down into his sleeve. "What the . . . ? Where did you get that dagger?"

"Argh!" the Gworf suddenly bellowed. He dropped Nell and grabbed his eye. Then he pulled his claw back and flung something against the wall.

"Pim!!!" Nell shrieked.

The Gworf, one eye squeezed shut, grabbed her again, furious now.

"I've had about enough of you!" he bellowed. He hugged her to his chest and squeezed. Nell gasped but could not breathe. The room started to fade. Then suddenly the Gworf's arms went slack and Nell was pulled free, just as the Gworf crumpled unconscious to the floor.

"Ock I weed ya yee," sang Sweet Baby, setting her down gently.

Nell hugged him. "Thank you, Sweet Baby," she whispered. "Thank you."

"Drop it," Nell heard Lord Taman say, "or I'll turn you into a frog." She could see Owen's dagger glinting dully in his hand. Lord Taman had his wand out. The two faced each other tensely, each waiting for the other to make the first move.

"Drop it, I said," Lord Taman repeated.

"Not on your life," said Owen.

"All right then. You asked for it," said Lord Taman. He pointed his wand. "Spirits of the swamp and bog," he began chanting, "change this foe—"

Nell launched herself at Lord Taman, diving at his knees.

"—into a frog!" he shouted as his feet went out from under him and he fell to one side, crashing into the wall.

Quickly Nell scrambled to grab one end of the wand. Lord Taman held on fiercely, and a sizzling hot jolt coursed through Nell's arm, knocking her backward against Owen.

Lord Taman jumped to his feet and loomed before Nell and Owen, a menacing silhouette against the back-light of the open cell door.

"Don't move," he said, brandishing the wand, "or I'll do you both in here and now."

And then Lord Taman's silhouette disappeared, swallowed up by a larger one.

"What the . . . let me go, you stupid oaf!" he yelled.

Sweet Baby had Lord Taman locked in a bear hug, his arms pinned against his sides.

"Hold him, Sweet Baby," Nell cried. "Don't let him go!"

Owen leapt forward, pressing the dagger against Lord Taman's Adam's apple.

"Drop the wand," he said.

Lord Taman struggled and grunted, but he did not release his grip on the wand.

"Drop it!" Owen demanded, pressing the dagger against Lord Taman's skin until a drop of blood oozed out.

Lord Taman's head lolled, then the wand fell from his grasp.

"Did you kill him?" Nell cried.

"No," said Owen. "Sweet Baby just squeezed the breath out of him. He fainted."

"Oh," said Nell, relieved. She bent to retrieve the wand and found herself eye level with Lord Taman's Charm Mark. It had been transformed into a cloven hoof—the symbol of Lord Graieconn! Lord Taman had entered into a covenant with the Lord of Darkness!"

"Do you *want* me to kill him?" Owen asked, still holding the dagger at Lord Taman's neck.

"No!" cried Nell. She looked at Lord Taman, and

despite his treachery could not hate him. He was her cousin after all, her flesh and blood.

"Why not?" asked Owen.

"Because . . . um . . . because we need him," said Nell, "to help us get out of here."

"How?" asked Owen.

"I haven't figured that out yet," said Nell. She waved the wand at Lord Taman. "Forge a chain of metal bright," she chanted. "Bind this foe and hold him tight."

A chain appeared, wrapping Lord Taman from neck to foot.

"Thank you, Sweet Baby," said Nell. "You can let him go now."

Sweet Baby released his hold, and Lord Taman dropped to the ground with a loud clank.

Owen tucked his dagger into his belt and turned to Nell.

"You sure you didn't grow up in the Lanes?" he asked. "You're mighty tough for a princess."

Nell smiled. "I've had a little help from my friends," she said. Then she gasped. "Which reminds me—Pim! Pim, where are you?"

There was no answer except the ever-present chirping and croaking. Nell's heart thumped. She remembered the awful sound of Pim's small body smacking against the wall and then dropping to the floor with a small splash. Could he have possibly survived?

"Owen," she said. "Get a torch from out in the stairwell. Hurry!"

"Pim?" Nell called again. "Where are you? Can you hear me?"

"Ribbet, ribbet, chirp," was the only answer.

Owen rushed back in with the torch and handed it to Nell. She lifted it high above her and surveyed the cell. Nothing. Could he have slipped beneath the water? Had he drowned?

"Hey," said Owen. "This is weird."

"What?" asked Nell.

"This frog has a beard," said Owen.

"What?" Nell came over and bent close.

Indeed one of the frogs peeking up out of the water had a bushy white beard hanging from its chin.

"Ribbet," said the frog.

"Oh, my!" cried Nell. "Lord Taman's frog spell! It must have hit Pim!"

"Ribbet, ribbet!" said the frog.

Nell reached down and carefully picked up the frog. Sure enough it was wearing a plaid vest and leather britches. But one of its legs dangled unnaturally.

"Pim?" Nell cried. "Are you all right?"

"Ribbet," said the frog.

"We've got to change him back, Owen," said Nell.

"Why?" asked Owen. "I kind of like him as a frog."

Nell shook her head impatiently. "I'm not kidding," she said. "I think he's hurt."

"Well, all right, then. Change him back."

Nell lifted Lord Taman's wand.

"But I've never undone a wand spell," she said. "What if I mess up? What if I hurt him?"

"Why don't we make the Wizard do it, then?" said Owen.

Nell shook her head again. "Are you crazy? I'm not about to give him back his wand."

"Mmm," said Owen. "Good point. Well, give me the wand then. We had a smattering of spell work at the academy. I can probably do it."

"Really? Are you sure?"

"No. But what's the alternative?"

Nell sighed. "All right," she said, handing over the wand and setting Pim down on a dry section of floor. "Just be *careful*."

Owen took the wand in his hand. "Nice one," he said, waving it dramatically.

"Ribbet," said the frog.

"Get on with it," said Nell. "We've got to get out of here!"

"All right, all right." Owen pointed the wand at Pim. "Spirits of the swamp and bog," he said, "change this frog into a log."

"Owen!" cried Nell.

There was a crackle of light, and there sat a log where Pim had been.

"Owen!" Nell raged. "I'm going to—"

"All right, all right," said Owen. "I was just playing around. Don't get your britches in a bunch!"

He pointed the wand again.

"Spirits of the swamp and bog," he said, "undo the log, undo the frog."

There were two crackles and then Pim stood glaring up at Owen, his hands on his hips.

"Hah!" he said, pointing a finger, "and *you* had the nerve to call *me* a lady!"

Nell looked at Owen and realized for the first time that he was still dressed as a princess. She giggled.

Owen narrowed his eyes and pointed the wand again.

"Told you I liked him better as a frog," he said.

Nell grabbed the wand out of his hand.

"Enough, you two!" She bent down close to Pim. "Your leg looks broken," she said. "Doesn't it hurt?"

"Of course it hurts," said Pim, "but Imps don't whine."

"No," said Owen. "Apparently they croak."

Nell rolled her eyes. "One more word," she warned, "and I turn you *both* into frogs. Now quit the nonsense and let's figure out how to get out of here!"

"Well, you know me," said Pim. "I tend to think the simple ideas work best."

"Is that because—" Owen started to tease, but Nell stomped on his toe.

"Go on, Pim," she said. "I'm listening."

"I say we just walk out of here," said Pim.

"Oh, yeah," said Owen. "They're just going to let us walk out of here."

"They will," said Pim, jerking a thumb at the still-unconscious Lord Taman, "if they think we're *his* prisoners."

Chapter Twenty-Five

The chain linked Nell, Owen, and Sweet Baby to Lord Taman. Pim's broken leg was splinted with Donagh Treeleaper's reed whistle. He rode in the cowl-like collar of Lord Taman's robe, with his sword gently pricking the Wizard's windpipe.

Don't even think of uttering a spell, Lord Taman had been warned, *or you'll be breathing through a hole in your neck.*

Nell had the wand tucked up her sleeve in case of emergencies. Not that she was really sure what she might do with it, but it gave her comfort.

They moved unchallenged through the chambers of Darkearth, Lord Taman obviously a familiar and respected member of the community. Nell was still stunned to think that someone she thought she knew so well could in fact be loyal to Graieconn. They emerged at last into the entrance cave where Darkearth's Dragons were housed.

Two Ghouls guarded the stable. Pim increased the

pressure on his sword until Lord Taman coughed. "Tell them we need a Dragon," Pim whispered, "and make it sound convincing."

"Lord Taman!" said one of the Ghouls. They both snapped to attention and raised their right hands in the sign of the cloven hoof.

Lord Taman responded in kind.

"A motley-looking crew you've got there," the first guard observed.

"Ay," said Lord Taman. "I'll be needing a transport worm. We're bound for the Oggle camp. They're in need of fresh flesh."

"Ah!" Both Ghouls laughed. "The young ones look sweet enough, but the big one'll be tough as leather."

"Ay," said Lord Taman, "but he'll feed a whole battalion."

"True enough." The second Ghoul chuckled. His partner disappeared into the stable, then returned leading a huge Bronze-wing with a cargo crate mounted behind its saddle.

Lord Taman led his three "prisoners" up a mounting ramp, released them from their chains, and opened the door of the crate.

"Get in there," he ordered, giving Owen a shove.

Pim pricked Lord Taman's neck with the sword as a reminder.

Nell and Sweet Baby followed Owen into the crate, then Lord Taman closed the door and climbed into the saddle.

"Tell the Oggles we hope they enjoy their dinner!" shouted the Ghouls as the Bronze-Wing lifted off.

It was quiet when they emerged from the cave, and Odom was still. Odomites were draped everywhere, sprawled in the gutters, slumped on the doorsteps, snoring on street corners. Miette's predictions had certainly been accurate.

The Bronze-wing was a strong flyer, and they quickly reached the ridge where Miette had promised to be waiting. Sure enough no sooner had they touched down than the girl peered cautiously out of a cave. At the sight of Lord Taman, she disappeared again.

Pim pricked Lord Taman. "Get out of the saddle, nice and easy," he said.

Nell pushed open the crate door and slid to the ground.

"Miette!" she said, hurrying over to the cave. "We're back. How is Beauty?"

There was no answer.

"Miette?" called Nell.

A hand reached out and pulled her into the darkness. "Hush," whispered Miette's voice. "Beauty is fine, but what are you doing with *him*?"

"Who?" asked Nell.

"Lord Taman," whispered Miette. "Graieconn's Chief Wizard."

"Chief Wizard?" Nell gasped. This was worse than she thought. How could Lord Taman have hidden such treachery from them all these years?

"Don't worry," said Nell. "He's our prisoner."

"Your *prisoner*?"

"Yes. Come on."

Nell pulled Miette out into the moonlight.

With Sweet Baby's help Owen had trussed Lord Taman with the chain again and stuffed a gag into his mouth. Nell reached up to help Pim down. He winced.

"You okay, Pim?" she asked. "You look awfully pale."

Pim mopped his brow. "Yeah," he said through gritted teeth. "I'll make it."

"Miette," said Nell. "You remember Pim?"

Miette nodded.

"And this is Owen and Sweet Baby," Nell continued.

"I know him," said Miette, pointing to Sweet Baby. "He's from Xandria, like me. His name is Gurit."

At the sound of his name Sweet Baby stopped singing and smiled. He patted his chest. "Urr," he repeated.

Nell smiled. "Nell," she said, patting her chest.

"Ell," Gurit mimicked.

Owen cleared his throat. "Are these introductions going to go on all night?" he asked, "or can we get out of here?"

"Isn't Owen a boy's name?" Miette asked with a look of confusion on her face.

"Yes, it's a *boy's* name," said Owen emphatically.

Miette shook her head. "Xandria must have sure changed since I was there," she said. "Back then the *girls* wore dresses and the *boys* wore trousers."

Nell laughed and Owen grimaced.

"Which reminds me," he said. "It's about time we switched back into our rightful clothes."

"Oh, no!" said Nell. "I'm not flying in a dress ever again!"

"But—"

"Sorry. No time for arguments," said Nell. "We've got to get going. Miette, do you think Beauty can fly again?"

"I think so," said Miette. "I fed and watered her before we left the stable, and she seemed okay on the flight up the mountain—just tired. She's been sleeping since we got here."

"All right," said Nell. "I'll ride Beauty. Owen, you take the Bronze-wing. The rest of you can ride in the crate."

"The rest?" said Owen. "You mean, we're taking *everybody* with us?"

"That's what I said," said Nell.

"But . . ." Owen glanced at Miette and Gurit. "Don't these Folk sort of . . . belong in Odom?"

Nell bristled. "*Nobody* belongs in Odom, Owen," she said, "and furthermore, you owe them your life."

Owen shrugged awkwardly. "All right," he said. "I just thought . . ."

"I know what you thought," said Nell, "and I don't like it."

"What about the Wizard?" Pim asked, his brow furrowed with pain.

Nell looked at him worriedly. "Are you sure you can make the trip, Pim?" she asked.

"I'll make it," said Pim between short, ragged breaths, "but the sooner we get going . . . the better. Now . . . what about the Wizard?"

"I don't know," said Nell, chewing her lip. "If we leave him, he could die up here before anyone finds him."

"Aw. Wouldn't that be too bad?" said Owen.

"For once . . . me and the boy are of the same . . . mind," said Pim. "He's . . . too dangerous an enemy to let live, Princess."

Nell swallowed hard. Owen and Pim were probably right, she realized, but she still cared for Lord Taman, still hoped that maybe, somehow, he could be won back from Lord Graieconn.

"I can't leave him," she said.

Owen shook his head. "Bad choice," he said.

Nell shrugged. "I'm sorry," she said. "I just can't."

Pim sighed. "All right," he rasped. "Let's load him . . . into the crate and get . . . out of here."

CHAPTER TWENTY-SIX

Beauty flew valiantly, though Nell could tell she was exhausted. The Bronze-wing lagged a bit behind, weighed down by his heavy load. They cleared the Mountains of Odom and passed over the plateau where Nell and Pim had made camp the day before. With any luck Nell guessed they would meet up with her father's army by dawn.

A couple of hours into the journey, Nell spied an encampment below. For a moment her heart sang, but then it lurched. It was not her father's army. It was the Oggles!

The Bronze-wing started moving up. Nell glanced back.

"What is it, Owen?" she yelled.

"Land!" came a sharp command.

Nell's head whipped around.

"Lord Taman!" she cried. "But how did you . . . ? Where's Owen?"

"You should have listened to your friends," said Lord Taman, sitting tall in the Bronze-wing's saddle. "The boy is in the crate now, enjoying a nap."

"But how—," Nell began.

"Never mind!" boomed Lord Taman. "I said, land!"

Panicked, Nell reached for the wand. It trembled in her hand. Instantly a ball of fire leapt from Lord Taman's hand to the wand, and a shot of lightning raced up her arm. With a cry she let the wand go, and it flew to Lord Taman's hand.

"Now, land!" he blared.

"Down, Beauty," said Nell.

Lord Taman threw back his head and laughed loud and long. "Now you see what you're up against," he said. "The power of Graieconn is unlimited!"

Nell's heart raced. She grabbed her mother's pendant. It pulsed and gave her courage. "Stay calm," she told herself. "Stay calm."

"Wake up, sleepy heads!" shouted Lord Taman, snapping his fingers at the crate as soon as the Dragons landed.

Miette shrieked and Nell heard Gurit grunt.

"What the . . . ?" Owen cried out. "What the clop is going on?"

Oggles quickly crowded around. They were terrible-looking creatures, with bloodred fangs and glowing yellow eyes.

"Good evening, my friends," said Lord Taman. "I've brought you a snack!"

Chills ran up Nell's spine as the Oggles all grunted with glee. One, presumably the leader, shouted orders and the rest began pulling the crate down from the Bronze-wing's back. They lifted it over their heads and carried it toward their campfire.

"You too," Lord Taman said, motioning Nell to the ground.

She slid from the saddle. Two Oggles grabbed her arms and started dragging her after the others. When they reached the fireside, the Oggles opened the crate and tossed her inside.

"What happened?" she whispered. "How did Lord Taman escape?"

"I don't know," said Owen. "First I was out there. Next thing I know, I'm in here."

"I'm afraid it's all my fault," said Pim contritely. "Miette and Gurit fell asleep and I tried hard to keep alert, but I guess the pain in my leg finally got to me. I blacked out, and Taman must have worked free of his gag. When I came to, he was out there and Owen was in here, asleep by my side—a spell apparently."

Nell sighed. "It's not your fault, Pim," she said. "It's mine. I should have listened to you and Owen, and left him back in Odom."

"I'd say I told you so," said Pim, "but somehow it would give me very little satisfaction under the present circumstances."

"What's going to happen to us?" asked Miette fearfully.

"I don't know," said Nell.

Gurit sat in a corner of the crate, hugging his knees and singing softly to himself.

A small group of Oggles began beating on drums and singing. The leader then led the rest in a dance around the campfire. Lord Taman stood beside the crate, watching it all and smiling. Nell looked up at him beseechingly.

"You're not really going to let them . . ."

"Eat you?" said Lord Taman. "Why not?"

"But . . . we're cousins," said Nell. "I love you, and Father loves you too. He even made you Grand Court Wizard."

Lord Taman snorted. "Grand Court *Servant* is more like it," he said. "Yes, sire. Right away, sire. Anything you say, sire. Ha! Those days are over. *I* will be King of Xandria soon."

"Is that what this is all about?" asked Nell. "Is that why you've turned against everything and everyone you ever cared about?"

"You know nothing of what I care about," said Lord Taman. "Now silence!"

He crossed his arms over his chest and leaned against the crate, the flickering firelight turning his skin to gold. The dancing went on and on, growing more and more frenzied.

"They're working up quite an appetite, I'd say," said Lord Taman with a chuckle, then he glanced skyward. "Ahh!" he said. "*More* friends to join in the festivities!"

Nell looked skyward too. Hundreds of Hillkin filled the air! She looked down at Pim.

He patted his whistle splint and smiled.

Chapter Twenty-seven

The dancing ended and the Hillkin mingled amiably with the Oggles. Donagh Treeleaper approached Lord Taman.

"My lord," he said, dipping his head respectfully. "We heard the drums of celebration and came to investigate. A surprise to find you here."

"Yes," said Lord Taman. "A surprise to me as well."

Donagh opened a pouch that hung at his waist and produced a clay pipe.

"Will you join me?" he asked Lord Taman. "The Hillkin are known for the quality of their smokeweed."

"Don't mind if I do," said Lord Taman.

Donagh filled the pipe with smokeweed and passed it to Lord Taman. Then he produced another for himself. Lastly he took a slender reed from his pouch, lit in the fire, and touched it first to Lord Taman's pipe, then to his own.

Lord Taman sucked deeply of the smoke.

"Ah," he said. "The Hillkin's reputation is well

deserved." He took another deep draught, then his body went limp and he tumbled to the ground.

"Now!" yelled Donagh.

Instantly the Hillkin unsheathed their knifelike claws and the smaller, unsuspecting Oggles were quickly subdued.

"The Hillkin will pay for this treachery!" the Oggle leader shouted.

"Tie them up!" commanded Donagh. He ripped the crate door open. "Hurry," he said to Nell and the others. "Fly east by south. You will find your father's army camped not far from here."

"How can we ever thank you?" asked Nell.

"Speak with your father," said Donagh. "The Hillkin will be needing new allies after tonight."

Nell nodded. "I owe you a great debt," she said. "I will do my best." She hurried after the others to where the two Dragons waited.

"Owen, you take Gurit," she said. "Miette and I and Pim will ride Beauty."

Owen nodded. "Mount," he yelled to the Bronze-wing. It lowered its head, and Owen helped Gurit climb aboard. Then he climbed up himself.

Nell did the same with Beauty, handing Pim over into Miette's care as she took up the reins.

"Away!" she shouted.

"Away!" Owen echoed, and they were airborne.

Nell waved to Donagh as the Oggle camp dropped away below.

"It won't be long now," Nell said over her shoulder. "How are you holding up, Pim?"

"I'm still with you, Princess!" shouted Pim. "We're a pair, don't forget!"

Nell smiled. The sky turned from black to deep purple to misty gray. Dawn was on its way. The stench of Odom was behind her, the sweet breath of the Hill Lands fresh in her face.

And then there were Dragons in the air, Dragons charging straight at them!

"Now what?" shouted Owen. "I'm not sure I can take too much more of this!"

Nell peered into the mists, hoping . . . hoping . . .

"Yes!" she cried. "It's the Dragonguard! Captain Kael! Captain Kael!"

The foremost of the Dragonguard raised his hand, giving the signal for the others to pull up.

"Princess!" he shouted. "Is it truly you?"

"Yes!" cried Nell. "Is my father safe?"

"Ay," said the captain, "but how is it that you fly from the direction of Odom?"

"I will explain it all," said Nell, "as soon as I see my father."

The Dragonguard escorted Beauty and the Bronze-wing to the ground. By the time they reached the campsite, news of the white Dragon had spread, and King Einar was running to meet them. His left leg was heavily bandaged, but it did not seem to slow him much. He grabbed Nell as soon as she slid from her saddle and whirled her in the air.

"My wild little girl," he said, laughing and crying at once. "You had me so worried! Where on Eldearth have you been?"

"Adventuring, Father," said Nell with a smile. She hugged him tight and kissed his cheek. "I have many stories to tell, but first there are some friends that you must meet." Her smile faded and she addressed her father sternly. "You must be very kind to them," she said quietly. "It is because of them that I have succeeded in my mission."

"What mission is that?" asked the King.

"This is Miette and Pim," said Nell, ignoring her father's question for the moment.

King Einar greeted Miette and reached up to help her down. "Where is the other?" he asked.

"HERE!" Pim shouted into the King's ear.

Nell laughed. "He's on Miette's shoulder," said Nell. "He's an Imp."

Just then Gurit appeared from behind Beauty.

"And this is Gurit," said Nell.

"Urr," said Gurit, patting his chest.

"Hello, Gurit," said King Einar. He glanced at Nell. "You certainly have an odd collection of friends," he mumbled.

Nell smiled. "Wonderfully odd," she said just as Owen ducked under Beauty's chin and strode up to the group. He bowed before King Einar.

"And last but not least," said Nell with a mischievous grin, "may I present your son, Owen."

The king's mouth gaped, and Owen looked over at Nell, his brow furrowed in confusion.

"What was that you just said?" Owen asked.

Nell giggled. "I didn't have a chance to tell you before this," she said, "but it turns out there's a reason we look so much alike."

Owen shook his head in bewilderment. "What are you talking about?" he asked.

"She is trying to tell you that you are her brother," said King Einar, "that you are my *son*." He had that sound in his voice again, that wondering awestruck joy.

Owen looked up at the king, then over at Nell again. "Have you all gone crazy?" he asked.

"No," said Nell. "There is much to explain."

"Yes," said the king, then he raised his head and looked around. "What of Lord Taman?" he asked. "Why is he not in your company?"

Nell's smile faded.

"As I said," she repeated, "there is much to explain."

Chapter Twenty-Eight

Nell started sending mind pictures as soon as the castle came into sight, hugs and kisses and gentle caresses.

"Please be all right," she whispered. "Minna, please be all right."

And then there was a tiny dot in the distance, a tiny dot growing larger, glowing purple in the sun. And then Nell was nearly knocked out of her saddle by a happy little Dragon, hurling itself into her arms, covering her face with slurpy Dragon kisses.

"Oh, Minna," she cried. "Minna, Minna, Minna!"

"Thrummm," sang the little creature in reply. "Thrummm, thrummm, thrummm."

The throne room was resplendent that evening, draped in velvet swags and satin ribbons, with flowers spilling from golden urns. Pim had a seat of honor, a specially made chair on a three-foot-tall pedestal. Across the aisle sat Miette and Gurit, their beaming mothers by their sides.

King Einar sat on his throne, with Nell and Owen occupying smaller identical thrones—one on his left and one on his right. Minna, who had not left Nell's side since her return, sat perched in her customary spot on the back of Nell's throne.

Owen still looked bewildered, and who could blame him? So much to absorb so quickly. His eyes sought out Lady Fidelia's in the crowded room and his "Auntie" smiled back at him, her eyes warm and glowing.

It was still hard for Nell, too, sharing her father's love and Lady Fidelia's, and the affection of all the court with this newcomer. She glanced over at him and he glanced back. Both blushed and looked down at their hands. It was hard getting used to, this new relationship. It would take time.

A dozen troubadours, spaced at intervals down both sides of the central aisle, lifted their horns to their lips. The long horns crossed, making an arch over the aisle, and the troubadours blew six notes announcing the beginning of the ceremony. Everyone stood, except for the three royals, and the injured Pim, who had been given special permission to remain seated.

Led by Captain Kael, the Royal Dragonriders entered the room in full dress uniform and proceeded toward the throne. Draped across his arms Captain Kael carried the pure white Montue mantle.

Nell swallowed hard, her emotions in a muddle.

There was no doubt who would be chosen to wear it. The whole kingdom had been abuzz since Owen's arrival. It was like a tremendous weight had been lifted off of everyone's shoulders. They were all so sure he was the Chosen One, so sure the prophecy would now be fulfilled, and so sure peace and harmony would soon be restored.

And if that was to be the case, then so be it. Why should she care? Let Owen bear the responsibility. He would make a good Imperial Wizard, she was sure.

Or was she?

If the truth be told, there were things about Owen that worried her. He needed some tempering, some wisdom, some compassion. But that was what the quest—and the apprenticeship—were about. Surely he would be ready when the time came. And as for her, she would not give up on her dreams of a brighter, better future for all the Folk of Eldearth. She resolved to continue her fight, doing her best to influence her powerful father and brother.

Captain Kael reached the base of the throne platform. He knelt, bowed his head, then stood again and held the mantle out to King Einar. King Einar accepted it, then he stood and turned to face Nell and Owen. His eyes brimmed with love and pride, and sorrow, too, for he understood better than they the burden he was about to bestow.

"Rise, my children," he said gently.

Nell and Owen stood. Nell squared her shoulders and lifted her chin, preparing herself to be gracious, to congratulate her brother and offer him her help and support.

King Einar lifted the mantle.

"Behold the Mantle of Trust," he said, "symbol of faith and pride, promise of power and responsibility."

Then in one sudden, sharp movement he ripped it in two. Nell's eyes went wide as he held half out to Owen, half out to her.

"It is for one far wiser than I to make this choice," he said. "I bestow the Mantle of Trust upon you both and with it, my love. Go forward, my children, and seek your destinies."

ABOUT THE AUTHOR

JACKIE FRENCH KOLLER is the author of more than thirty books for children and young adults, including the popular Dragonling fantasy series, available in a two-volume collector's set. Her books have garnered numerous awards and honors from the American Library Association, the International Reading Association, and many others, and have been published in several foreign languages. One of her novels was made into the movie *You Wish* for the Disney Channel. Ms. Koller, mother of three grown children, now lives on a mountain in western Massachusetts with her husband, George, and her black Lab, Cassie. She welcomes visitors to her Web site: http://www.jackiefrenchkoller.com.